DRAMARAMA

DRAMARAMA

E. Lockhart

HYPERION/NEW YORK

Printed in the United States of America
First Edition
1 3 5 7 9 10 8 6 4 2
This book is set in 12-point Adobe Garamond.
Designed by Elizabeth H. Clark
Reinforced binding

Library of Congress Cataloging-in-Publication Data
Lockhart, E.
p.   cm.
Summary: Spending their summer at Wildewood Academy, an elite
boarding school for the performing arts, tests the bond between
Sadye and her best friend, Demi.
ISBN-13: 978-0-7868-3815-8
ISBN-10: 0-7868-3815-9
[1. Actors and actresses—Fiction. 2. Best friends—Fiction.
3. Friendship—Fiction. 4.
High Schools—Fiction. 5. Schools—Fiction.] I. Title.
PZ7.L79757Dra 2006
[Fic]—dc22
2006049599

Visit www.hyperionbooksforchildren.com

*For Big Len, who gave me all those albums
and took me to all those shows*

TRANSCRIPT of a microcassette recording:

Demi: Is it on?

Sadye: That red light is supposed to glow.

Demi: It *is* glowing.

Sadye: No, it's not.

Demi: Yes, it is. You can't see because of the angle.

Sadye: Stop it and check.

(thump thumpy thump, click click)

Demi: Ha-HA! Let the record show that I was right.

Sadye: *(silence)*

Demi: Come, now. Give me some credit. The light was way on.

Sadye: *(all fancy)* Let's begin, *shall* we?

Demi: Of course, darling. But I was right.

Sadye: Here goes. It is June twenty-fourth, and we, Douglas B. Howard Junior--

Demi: Demi!

Sadye: --known to those who love him as Demi--

Demi: *(interrupting)*--and Sarah Paulson, known to those who worship and lust after her as Sadye--

Sadye: Correction: known only to herself and Demi as Sadye--

Demi: *(interrupting again)*--that's SAY-dee, s-a-d-y-e, and don't you spell it wrong 'cause she's gonna be famous one day--

Sadye: --are here in the back of the Paulson minivan--

Demi: --talking into a teeny-weeny journalist-type cassette recorder.

Sadye: Micro.

Demi: Talking into a microcassette recorder to document the all-important fact that we are *leaving* Brenton, Ohio.

Sadye: Wooo-hooo!

Demi: We do *not* have to live in that Brenton suckiness for eight whole weeks.

Sadye: Good-bye, oh, dowdy math teachers! Good-bye, oh, mean cheerleaders! Good-bye, no-neck jock contingent, boring do-gooders, and juvenile delinquents!

Demi: Good-bye, stupid shopping mall! Good-bye, awful hairstyles!

Sadye: Good-bye, shallow, vacant members of the junior class and flat green lawns of suburbia! Good-bye, good-bye, and good riddance!

Demi: *(singing)* If ya don't mind having to live in Brenton . . . it's a fine life!

Sadye: *(singing backup)* It's a fine life!

Demi: If ya don't mind prejudice, pain, and boredom . . . it's a fine life!

Sadye: It's a fine life!

(Obvious and intentional parental

coughing from the front seat of
the minivan, where Sadye's dad
is driving.)

Mr. Paulson: A little less noise
from the peanut gallery, thank
you.

Sadye: Sorry, Dad.

Demi: Sorry, Mr. Paulson. It was
Oliver!.

Sadye: *Oliver!*, the Brenton version.

Mr. Paulson: Oliver or no Oliver,
you two are blowing my ears out.

Demi: Hey, do we have the new
Broadway cast album in here?

Sayde: I think so. I packed it.
Dad, can you find it?

Mr. Paulson: What?

Sadye: The *Oliver!* CD. Duh.

(Mr. Paulson puts the CD in the
minivan stereo)

Demi: I used to be a boy soprano.

Sadye: We know, we know.

Demi: Now I have to do it in
falsetto.

(He attempts to sing a few bars of
"Food, Glorious Food" along with
the boy sopranos of the Oliver!
cast)

Sadye: Give it up, darling. You sound like Frankie Valli.

Demi: I'll take that as a compliment.

Sadye: Hah!

Demi: What? I love *Jersey Boys*. I'm all about *Jersey Boys*.

Sadye: Frankie Valli on crack.

Demi: Oh, shush your mouth. I'll be the first black man to play Frankie on Broadway. You watch me.

(They ride in silence for a minute. Demi eats potato chips out of a bag.)

Demi: Three more hours, and we'll be in heaven.

Sadye: Wildewood.

Demi: Like I said. Heaven.

Sadye: You're messing our tape up! Posterity will be confused.

Demi: Okay, say it right, then.

Sadye: Demi and I will be attending the Wildewood Academy of Performing Arts, Summer Theater Institute, 2005.

Demi: We are gonna take over that place. Absolutely rule it.

Sadye: You think?

Demi: Oh, yeah. We'll be stars.

Sadye: Don't be underconfident, now.

Demi: Ha-ha.

Sadye: Your lips are chapped.

Demi: We will. Be. Stars. I am predicting it, and I will make it so.

Sadye: I said, your lips are chapped.

Demi: Are you trying to deflate my ego? Because it will *not* be deflated.

Sadye: *(laughs)*

Demi: That thing is puncture-proof, baby.

Sadye: No, really. You need some lip balm.

Demi: Do you have? Give it here. Ooh, green apple flavor.

Sadye: Turn off the microcassette. We've degenerated.

Demi: True. All of posterity does not need to hear about my chapped lips.

(click)

Demi.

My coconspirator. My first true friend. A spirit made of equal parts ambition and razzle-dazzle. A big baritone that slides easily into falsetto. And a future as bright as the lights on 42nd Street.

Demi believed that the Wildewood Summer Institute would be heaven. Believed he would be king there, and I would be queen, and we would live all summer in utter fabulousness.

And he was right—about himself, at least.

In Brenton, Ohio, where I'm from, committing suicide would be redundant. It's a nothing town, as lacking in character as Cream of Wheat. Before I met Demi, the only time I ever felt alive was when I took tap and jazz at Miss Delilah's School of Dance in Cleveland twenty miles away—three weekday afternoons plus Saturday mornings. At Miss Delilah's there was music, pizzazz, glitter. Show tune medleys and old Miss D. with her feather boa and varicose veins yelling "Five, six, seven, eight!"—beaming when we nailed a tap routine.

When the music ended and the ninety minutes were up, all the kids from dance class would throw on sweatshirts and run outside to waiting cars. They lived in the city. But I'd stay after class and wipe handprints off the sticky mirrors, listening to Miss Delilah and Mr. Trocadero (the jazz teacher) talk about shows they'd done when they were young, or plays they'd seen on Broadway. Eventually, they'd shut off the lights and lock the studio doors—and I'd be forced to go wait on the street corner for the last bus back to Brenton.

My home life wasn't awful. It was just dead. Seriously razzle-dazzle deprived.

I am an only child and my father is old. Sixty-six. Retired. My mother is his second wife, and she's not old at all, comparatively. But she's deaf. She speaks pretty clearly, and reads lips, but she also uses ASL—American Sign Language. She works for a kitchen supplies catalog.

So our house is quiet. No one yells from room to room. People rarely talk when they can sign. There's hardly ever any music or television on.

My mom works, thinks about work, and talks about work with occasional forays into cooking; my dad, who used to be a banker, prunes peony bushes and mows the lawn, belongs to a golf and tennis club, and reads books on the Civil War.

Me, I don't fit in. Not in my family. And not at school.

Before Demi, I hung around at lunchtime with

some bland girls who were friendly enough: Dora, Ada, and Laura. Short, feminine girls who tolerated my occasional deviations from standard Brenton High casual wear and let me borrow their notes if I was out sick.

But we weren't really friends.

I was pizzazz when they were pretty; I was a big-nose broad when they were all pint-size mommy trackers; I was a Great Dane and they were all Westies; I was mint chocolate chip when they were all vanilla—and yet I didn't want to be like them.

A sample lunch conversation in Dora-Ada-Laura-land:

"Hey, did you guys bring umbrellas?"

"No, I didn't. I hope it doesn't rain."

"Me too. I hate rain."

"Rain, rain, go away, come again some other day!"

"Check out my umbrella, it's so cute!"

"Cute."

"So cute."

"Don't you hate rain?"

"I so hate it."

"I like it when it's sunny. What do you guys think?"

"Oh, sunny is definitely the best. Cute umbrella, though, Dora."

I felt worse *with* them than I did without them,

and the only way I kept from losing my mind due to razzle-dazzle deprivation and profound loneliness was to spend all my free time watching musicals on DVD. My favorites were *Chicago, Singin' in the Rain, Sweet Charity, Damn Yankees, Kiss Me Kate, West Side Story, An American in Paris,* and of course, *Cabaret*—the best movie ever made. An unbelievable 128 minutes of fabulousness.

"You'll turn your brain to gelatin watching all that television," my father said to me one day.

"It's not television," I said. "It's *Cabaret*. One of the greatest musicals of all time."

"Looks like a television to me." He knocked the top of the set. "Yep. Definitely a television. Oh, and there's my daughter on the couch, when it's a beautiful sunny day outside."

"It was directed by Bob Fosse," I said. "Liza Minnelli won best actress."

"Sarah."

"What?"

"I'm going to walk down to the store to get some stuff for dinner. Come with me, will you? At least get a little fresh air."

"Fine." I pushed the pause button.

When we got home, though, I sat right back on the couch and watched the end of *Cabaret*. Because it was a song, filling up the silence of my life.

Before Demi, and before Wildewood, I felt too tall to fit in my own house. Too tall to fit in my own school. To big for Brenton.

It wasn't about my height—though I'm five foot ten. It was like I was this supersonic, hydrophonic, gigantic person—only no one could see it. Like I had an undiscovered superpower. Like I was in a chrysalis, and when I popped out everyone would be shocked at my beauty and the breadth of my wings. Like there was a sound track to my life, and it was always blasting. But everyone in the world was deaf, except me.

I know that doesn't make sense. What I'm trying to say is that sometimes I felt like the extra five inches I had on most girls was a symptom of the bigness inside me.

Something that needed expression. That would explode if I didn't let it out.

A Lurking Bigness.

Demi Howard was the first person who could ever see it.

To everyone else, I was just Sarah. But to him, I was Sadye.

*   *   *

In early February, there was an announcement posted on the bulletin board at Miss Delilah's.

Close your eyes and imagine . . . a summer filled with the magic of theater! One of the nation's only full-time performing arts boarding schools is pleased to present the 28th year of its summer program.

Everyone is cast in a show. You will study dance, voice, pantomime, and acting with theater professionals.

Wildewood Academy for the Performing Arts
Summer Theater Institute
Students ages 15–18

Auditions in major cities.
February 19, Cleveland Rehearsal Halls, 1 P.M.
Applicants: Prepare a song (16 bars) and a monologue (2 minutes). You will learn a dance combination.

Wildewood. I repeated the name to myself, under my breath, as I wrote down the information.

Wildewood. Wildewood.

I had only a week to get ready.

* * *

"Popular" (from *Wicked*) had been on repeat every day for a month, so choosing a song was easy enough. I knew every phrase, every breath, every note. And for the monologue, I asked Miss Delilah's advice after class the next Wednesday. She gave me the balcony scene from *Romeo and Juliet*, saying it was perfect for a girl my age, and the directors would be impressed with a classical choice. "Emote!" Miss Delilah cried, clutching my arm. "Make it passionate! Do it like this!" She inhaled and began to play Juliet herself:

> O ROmeo, Romeo! wherefore ART thou ROmeo?
>   *(looking around in frenzy)*
> DeNY thy father *(shaking fist)* and refuse thy name!
>   *(panting, as if collecting wits after great exertion)*
> Or, if thou wilt NOT, *(gazing down sorrowfully
>   and modestly)* be but SWORN MY LOVE,
>   *(loud and ecstatic)*
> And I'll no LONGer be a Capulet. *(heroic!
>   clenching fist)*

I took the book Miss Delilah gave me, memorized the lines, and practiced in my room. "DeNY thy father" *(shake fist)* "and refuse thy name!" *(pant)*—but whenever I spoke the words that way, my voice sounded phony in my head, and my gestures felt false.

All that ecstasy and fist-shaking—it had razzle-dazzle all right, so why did it feel wrong?

I asked my mother to watch me do the monologue. She sat politely on a stool in the kitchen while I spoke, but I could see her eyes darting to her open laptop and her "to do" list. She clapped when I was done. "I love you, Sarah," she said. "I hope you get the part."

"Arggggh!"

"What?" My mother looked genuinely puzzled.

"You're not saying anything!"

"What else shall I say?"

I signed at her: "You're not even watching! You're supposed to say something!"

"I said, I hope you get the part."

"It's not a part!" I stamped my foot.

"Then what is it?"

"It's the summer institute. I told you about it already."

"Oh." She looked apologetic. "I'm sorry."

I felt bad. "So tell me what you think, then."

My mom paused, as if pondering some deep comment she was going to make about Juliet's emotions. "I think," she finally said, "that it's wonderful to see you getting involved in a new hobby."

I did the monologue for my dad the next day. He said it was great and he was so proud, and did I know where Verona was? Because he could show it to me on the globe upstairs if I wanted.

I let him show me, and that was the end of our conversation.

THE SATURDAY before the Wildewood audition, I went to the hair salon on Garden Place. A middle-aged man with silly blond curls said he was free to take me as a walk-in customer.

"Cut it off!" I told him, shaking my long hair out of its ponytail.

"Are you sure?"

"To the chin."

"That's a big change."

"And bangs, with the back angled up."

"You have pretty hair," the stylist said. "It's so feminine. How's about we do a layered cut, something soft, and only take it up to the middle of your back, give it some movement?"

All the girls at Brenton have long hair. Soft hair with some layers for movement. "I'm over being feminine," I answered. "No offense."

My long, dark brown hair fell to the hardwood floor of the salon. When he was finished, the girl in the mirror looked older. Glam.

I walked out of the shop, and the wind blew sleety snow like it does in February. I took the bus to Cleveland and went to the vintage clothing shop I used to sometimes browse around in before dance class. I had my holiday money in my pocket—$350.

I bought two suede miniskirts, knee-high boots, a bone-colored leather jacket, two vintage dresses, and four T-shirts with logos like KENTUCKY HOME FOR THE CRIMINALLY INSANE. Plus two glitter barrettes, a pair of purple cords, red flats with pointy toes, and a sweater covered in sequins.

I shoved my jeans and my soft, blue sweater (typical Brenton-wear) into a plastic bag and went home in something outrageous.

I felt like I didn't know myself anymore.

Deny thy father and refuse thy name.

WHEN I ARRIVED at the auditions, there were teenagers sprawled everywhere. On the floor, on benches, leaning against the walls. They were stretching and doing vocal warm-ups. A few bored-looking parents read newspapers and magazines at one end of the hall. Piano music thudded from behind a door.

I found a spot on the floor and pulled out the text of my monologue, which I had written out on a piece of notebook paper. "O ROmeo, Romeo! wherefore ART thou, ROmeo?"

A boy sat down beside me.

Douglas Howard.

I knew who he was. He was new this year, and I'd noticed him eating lunch alone at Brenton High. He had dark skin and a closely shaved afro, but he never hung out with the small clique of African American students at our school. In fact, he didn't seem to hang out with anyone. He hardly ever talked in class.

Every time I'd seen him before, he'd been wearing dark, nondescript clothes. Jeans and a sweatshirt. But not today. Today, Douglas Howard was decked out in a skintight silver shirt over red workout pants, and he had a bowler hat on his head.

He elbowed me in the ribs, laughing and accusing. "You! You go to Brenton."

"Yeah," I said. "I've seen you around."

He was lean but built—I could see the muscles of his legs through the thin fabric of his pants. A high-boned face, wide eyes, and a full mouth. The skin on his cheeks was bumpy where he was starting to need to shave, and he flashed a wide grin. "Douglas Howard, Jr. But you should call me Demi."

"Demi?"

"Like demitasse. Or demi-plié. Or demimonde. But not like Demi Moore."

"Got it."

"It comes from being a junior. My whole family calls me that. Like I'm half the man my father is. Get it? Very funny, ha-ha. But it's better than Douglas, so I keep it."

I rolled my eyes and held out my hand. "Sarah Paulson."

"Hmm. I don't think so," Demi said.

"What?"

"Not with that hair."

"I just cut it."

"I know. Did anyone ever tell you you look like Liza Minnelli?"

And that, in Demi's universe, is the highest compliment in the world. Because Demi loves Liza. He kind of wants to *be* Liza. Not Liza now. Liza from back when she was winning Academy Awards and starring on Broadway—an odd, vulnerable creature who danced like a black cat and belted like a bugle.

I jumped up, grabbed the wooden chair next to me, snatched the bowler hat off Demi's head, and hit the pose from the *Cabaret* poster: one foot on the seat of the chair, the other leg extended, hat shading my eyes.

"Oh, you're *perfect*!" Demi cried. "I love you!"

"It's the best movie."

"The best. That's what life is, right? A cabaret."

"A cabaret."

We were silent for a moment. I sat back down.

"I know what you're thinking," Demi announced.

"Do not."

"Do, too. Let me tell you."

"Go for it."

"You are thinking, where did this hot black boy in a silver shirt come from? Because I have seen that kid at school and he does *not* look anywhere near as good as he looks today."

"I was thinking about Juliet," I said. "But that was a close second."

"Juliet? She's only fourteen. Don't waste your energy trying to figure *her* out."

I laughed.

"I'm biding my time," said Demi. "That's the answer."

"What do you mean?"

"Until I can get to New York. I just go to school, do my homework, and wear my invisible straight-boy drag. No one sees me. No one hears me. No one talks to me. That way, no prejudiced, homophobic football player decides to kick the stuffing out of me in the locker room."

I nodded. Listening to Demi was like sticking my arm in a socket. I felt this jolt of something—joy, kinship, something—that I didn't remember ever having felt before, not even in tap class.

"That badness happened to me last year when we lived in Michigan, and there is no way I'm letting it happen again," he went on.

"Got it," I said. "They won't hear it here."

"Okay, then. Enough about me," said Demi, reaching up and touching my hair under his bowler hat. "Let's go back to your name."

"What's wrong with my name?"

"Sarah? Please."

"What?"

"Sarahs are dull and mild and small and pretty," said Demi. "Are you dull and mild and small and pretty?"

I had to admit that I was not. But in Brenton, it had always seemed like a problem.

"No," he went on. "You are . . . Let me see. You are . . ."

"Tall."

"Tall. Yes. And full of attitude. And I can't call you

pretty, not with that nose," he said. "But you are . . . dramatic."

"Wait, are you disparaging my nose?"

"No, 'dramatic' is too basic. You are . . . gawky-sexy. That's it."

"I'm what?"

"Gawky-sexy. And that means that you are *not* Sarah."

Hm.

Demi had already made it clear that he was gay. But still it felt good to have him say those things. Even with the crack about my nose, he seemed to appreciate who I was, *precisely*. Like he really saw me.

With the Lurking Bigness inside.

It was like we fell in love a little, just then. Even though we didn't.

"You think Frances Gumm was content to go through life with a stupid name like that when all her saucy amazingness was dying to get out?" Demi asked. "No. She changed her name to—"

"Judy Garland," I interrupted.

"Very good. And what about Norma Jean Baker?"

"Marilyn Monroe."

"See?" Demi argued. "That's all the difference in the world. Norma Jean. Marilyn. One is a nice librarian. The other is a sex goddess."

I still had his bowler hat, so I tilted it rakishly. "What should my name be?"

"Sarah. Sarah . . ." he mused. "What are the nick-names?"

"I don't know. Sally. Sarie?"

"No, something more exotic. Serenity. Or Zarah, maybe."

"Sadie, that's another one. I like that, actually."

Demi looked at me appraisingly. "Sadie. That could suit you. Only, you should be Sadye with a *Y*, like Liza with a *Z*."

"Spell it for me."

"S-a-d-y-e."

It sounded dramatic and funny and gawky-sexy. "Okay, that's it. I'm her," I said with finality. I pulled my Wildewood application form out of my bag, and found a pen.

Sarah, crossed out. And Sadye, written in.

SOMEONE OFFICIAL made an announcement. They would call us into the studio one at a time. We had two minutes for the monologue, sixteen bars for the song, plus a minute for question and answer. At four o'clock we were all to reappear for the dance audition.

Demi went third. He was doing a dramatic monologue from *Top Dog/Underdog* and a song from *Hair*.

Thing was, during the first two auditions we hadn't been able to hear any sound beyond the dull thump of the piano through the closed door. But when Demi sang, every note came through.

He did "Manchester, England," the song where Claude fantasizes (or lies) that he's from Manchester rather than Flushing, New York, because he thinks it sounds better. He calls himself a "genius genius," and believes in himself so much that he figures even God believes in him.

The song was very Demi, all the way through. Even just knowing him an hour, I could tell. He belted the number out so large that everyone in the hallway shut up and listened. He coasted through the high notes like they were sweet air.

He finished. Then silence through the door, while they asked him questions.

Demi came out and collapsed theatrically on the floor of the hallway.

"You nailed it," I told him.

"You could hear me?"

"Oh, yeah."

He glanced at the closed door, through which we could hear nothing besides the thump of the piano on the low notes as the next person sang. "I must be serious loud, then, right?"

"Mm-hm."

"Well, loud is good," said Demi. "Wildewood, here I come, baby."

For the next hour, Demi and I chatted about *Rent* and Brenton High and what we thought Wildewood would be like if we got in—but I wasn't concentrating anymore. I was panicking. Juliet on the balcony was now not even a fraction of my problem. Because if you had to sing like Demi to get into Wildewood, then I hadn't a chance.

If you've heard the sound track to *Wicked*, you know that "Popular" is performed by a tiny, blond bombshell (Kristin Chenoweth) with an incredible voice that veers from comically nasal to effortlessly high and clear. The song is funny: Galinda, future Glinda the "Good" Witch of the North, is offering a makeover to the homely, green-skinned Elphaba, future Wicked Witch of the West.

My own version had sounded okay when I sang it in the shower. I had concentrated on making my voice sound bouncy and clear like Kristin's, and though I had to admit the high notes were hard for me to reach, I thought the overall effect was pretty good.

But now, after hearing Demi, I knew it wasn't working. Why on earth had I picked a song written for a four-foot-eleven opera-trained blonde?

I thought about my small voice coming out of my big gawky body. My strained high notes. My utter lack of bouncy, Kristinish clarity. "I should shoot myself now," I said, interrupting Demi.

"What? Why?"

"Look at me. I am not remotely Kristinish. I need a different song."

He knew what I meant immediately. "What are you doing?" he demanded. "*Charlie Brown* or *Wicked*?" (Kristin won a Tony for playing Sally in *You're a Good Man, Charlie Brown*.)

"'Popular.'"

"Okay." Demi was all business. "Here's what you've got to remember. You're not Kristin."

"Duh."

"No, don't say duh. I mean, no one is Kristin. And true, you're not even Kristin*ish*. But that doesn't matter, because those people in there don't want to see you trying to be Kristin, even if you could be as Kristinish as Kristin herself. They want to see Sadye, and find out what Sadye can do."

"I don't sing like you do, believe me."

"Well," Demi vamped, "no one does. But you should work what you've got. The way you work that nose."

I socked him on the arm.

"I'm serious," Demi said. "You're like Barbra." (He meant Streisand). "You take a nose that would be ugly on lots of other girls, and you make it fabulous."

He thought I was working my nose. And maybe I was. "So?" I asked.

"So. Do that with your voice."

HALF AN HOUR later, my name was called. My throat felt tight and my palms were wet. I went in, clutching my application and sheet music.

Sitting at a table were three adults. Ordinary white grown-ups in jeans and sweaters—two women and a round, disheveled man with a brown beard. Someone reached a hand out for my application, and motioned for me to give the sheet music to the piano player. "Sadye Paulson. Start with the monologue."

"Juliet on the balcony," I said, and the man with the beard snorted. As if he'd heard the same speech three times already that day.

I took a deep breath and thought about what Demi had said.

Work what you've got.

Show what Sadye can do.

And I realized, as I spoke the first words, that the way Miss Delilah had acted out the scene might be good; it might be what these Wildewood people were looking for; might be real acting—but it wasn't what I could offer. I had never taken an acting class, and there was no way I could reach pinnacles of conflicting emotions in the space of two minutes without being fake.

So I spoke it. Like I was talking. Like it was as natural to say "Wherefore art thou Romeo?" as it would be to say "Why do you have to be named Romeo, of all things?"

I didn't do any of the gestures I had rehearsed. I left my arms down at my sides and said the words, thinking—not about Romeo, or some imaginary boyfriend, as I'd tried to do before when I'd rehearsed—but about something I wanted.

Juliet and I both wanted something badly. She wanted to be with Romeo. And I wanted to go to Wildewood with Demi.

"Thank you," said the man with the beard when I had finished. "Do the song now." His voice was higher than you'd expect from a person his size, and there was no emotion or encouragement in it.

The piano player banged straight into the chorus. I had practiced the song with cute, small, Kristinish movements that allowed me to sing as loudly and clearly as I could manage—but I had to change what I'd planned or I'd never get in.

I grabbed Demi's bowler hat off a folding chair where I had put it when I entered—flipped it up my arm onto my head (a trick I'd learned in tap class), and struck a pose.

I couldn't sing like Kristin—so what? I wouldn't try. I would do what *I* could do. What Sadye could do.

I growled that bouncy soprano number out—talking over the music in the most anti-Kristinish voice I could manage.

I was ironic, I was condescending, I was authoritative. I was probably a little ridiculous and weird.

And I danced. Some Bob Fosse knockoff I made up as I went along.

And while I was doing it—for those sixteen bars—I didn't think. I didn't think about how my voice sounded, or what feelings I was supposed to feel, or how I had to take a breath after "flirt and flounce" in order to get to the end of the line.

I just performed.

When I was done, I felt a bizarre mix of shame and exultation.

Had I been brilliant, or had I been a fool?

The faces of the interviewers were blank.

At least, I thought, I did something memorable.

I *did* something just now. Something Sadye.

I wasn't home watching musicals on television. I was here, letting my Lurking Bigness out.

"Thank you," the man said coolly. "Now, Miss Paulson, tell us why you want to attend Wildewood next summer."

I had known they'd ask me this; Demi told me. And I'd meant to say that I hoped to learn the craft of musical theater and be part of a community.

Instead, I blurted, "I want to get out of Ohio."

And they all laughed.

I FELT A BIT hysterical, after. Not knowing if I'd completely bombed—or nailed it. Demi suggested we go out for sandwiches, and we got soaked in a sudden downpour. But instead of hurrying through the wet with my shoulders up around my ears as I usually did, I danced and splashed in the puddles. Showing off to cover my nerves.

Demi laughed and belted out "Singin' in the Rain," grabbing my hands and twirling me down the sidewalk.

We found a Blimpie and went in, still singing. Customers with damp hair and sour faces looked up from their lunches, scowling. But we didn't care. We were like balls of sunshine brightening up the Blimpie.

We got drinks.

We ordered meatball subs.

For Demi's amusement, I made up the following work of questionable genius:

Meatball, oh meatball,
you're a small round lump of meat (meat meat!)
Soaking in your sauce, you are
a treat I plan to eat (eat eat!)

It's true, you are faintly repulsive
if I think about you too much.
You're probably full of elbows and eyeballs,
knuckles and entrails and such.
The meatball chef has ground up all
the things that should be waste,
and so . . .
I shouldn't analyze you, or
I won't enjoy your taste!

Meatball, oh meatball,
you're a small round lump of meat (meat meat!)
Soaking in your sauce, you are
a treat I plan to eat (eat eat!)

Stephen Schwartz, eat my dust.

The Blimpie manager politely asked us to keep it down, but we completely failed to do it. We were ejected for harmonizing about the questionable contents of the company's meat products, and forced into the rain. We ate the rest of our subs under the awning, and dashed back for the dance audition.

(click)

Sadye: It's *still* June twenty-fourth.

Demi: And we are *still* in the car.

Sadye: There is so, so, so much traffic.

Demi: Traffic like for miles.

Sadye: And we have to pee.

Demi: We trashed the back of the minivan. Sadye spilled her corn nuggy things.

Sadye: Demi sang all of *Rent* until we made him shut up. He sang "Tango: Maureen" all by himself.

Demi: With distinctive character

voices! And Sadye did
interpretive dance.

Sadye: *While* wearing my seat belt,
no less!

Demi: Safety first, that's our
motto. You outdid yourself on
"Seasons of Love."

Sadye: Thank you.

Demi: Of course.

Sadye: Anyway, we turned on the
recorder again because we want
to state our goals for
Wildewood. So we can listen
back at the end of the summer
and see if we achieved
them.

Demi: Okay, so what are your
goals, Miss Sadye?

Sadye: I want to get a part with
actual lines.

Demi: You are selling yourself so
short. Shorty Shortson, that's
you now.

Sadye: All right . . . Hm.

Demi: Go on. Bust out with it.

Sadye: I want to learn to sing.

Demi: Good. And what else?

Sadye: I want to figure out if I'm

any good at this stuff. Like if
I deserve to be there.

Demi: *(laughing)* My only goal is
total domination.

Sadye: Hello!

Demi: That's really what I want to
accomplish.

Sadye: You know what I think?

Demi: What?

Sadye: Not about total domination.
About what you should do this
summer?

Demi: What?

Sadye: I think you should find
love.

(click)

AFTER THE AUDITIONS, Demi and I took the bus
home together. And we never parted again.

He lay low at school—his invisibility routine
perfected. We ate lunch together, and laughed at the
cheerleaders together, and passed each other notes in
the hallways.

People assumed we were a couple.

And in a way, we were.

I wasn't the Kristinish, vanilla-type of girl who appealed to Brenton boys, and once I met Demi, no one even looked at me. Because I was taken. He called me all the time, ate dinner with my parents, took me to the movies, bought me presents, and really, did most of the things a boyfriend would do. I hardly thought about anyone else.

For his part, it wasn't like there was any competition for his attentions. Demi had known he was gay in fifth grade, and told his parents in tenth. But he'd never had a boyfriend. His lack of romance was a combination of minimal opportunity and parental disapproval. His dad was a lawyer and his mom did something with bonds. When he told them he was gay, his mother embraced him with a tight fake hug, and his dad patted him on the shoulder and said, "You're our son and we accept you"—like they'd suspected it for a while. He saw a well-thumbed copy of *When Your Child Is Homosexual: A Coping Guide for Loving Parents* in the trunk of his mother's car a few days later.

Thing was, the acceptance wasn't real. I could see it when I went over to Demi's house. I had dinner with his parents lots of times, and while his dad would be perfectly charming—telling stories about some ball game he'd gone to or some hilarity that had happened at his office party—as soon as he had to actually interact with Demi, he became this tight, false person, with nothing to say. He stretched a smile across his mouth and forced himself to pat Demi on the shoulder, but you could tell he thought his son was a limp napkin of a boy instead of the hetero breeder he'd been hoping for, and that he was simulating affection and comfort, instead of feeling them.

Mrs. Howard was the same. Being in that house was like being in a bad sitcom. Good-looking people told amusing jokes, the decor was nice, and the living room bigger than most people's—but no one was relating to each other. No one seemed like a real person.

So Demi knew that an actual flesh-and-blood boyfriend—even if he could find one in razzle-dazzle–deprived Brenton—would shatter the house of ice he lived in. His parents were only okay with him being gay so long as they never had to know anything about it.

Me, at least I had parents who—though boring—actually meant it when they said they loved me.

Demi had no one.

That's why in the car, I said Demi needed to find love. Looks, brains, money, talent: everything else, he already had.

* * *

You don't spend eight years taking your kid to jazz and tap lessons without meeting some gay people. My parents lived life on the straight and narrow path, but they had long since got used to the idea of homosexuality. The jazz teacher at Miss Delilah's, Mr. Trocadero, was flamboyant, and they'd known him for years.

They liked Demi fine, and though at first he did his invisible straight-boy routine around them, soon it became clear that they never got worked up over anything, and in fact, barely noticed whether he was there or not—so he might as well be himself.

Of course, Demi hates not to be noticed unless he's trying to be invisible on purpose, so soon it became a game with us—to see if he and I could make them laugh or jolt them out of their small, even-tempered mode of relating. But it never worked. They saw him (and me) as rowdy animals of minimal interest.

The teenagers are jumping on the couch. Sigh. I'll read the paper in the armchair, then.

The teenagers are attempting to stage *Godspell* wearing pillowcases on their heads. Well, let them enjoy themselves while I pay some bills at the kitchen table.

The teenagers are singing songs about meatballs at top volume during dinner. Hm. This is good tomato sauce. Honey, did you buy a new brand?

The teenagers are choreographing halfway porno-graphic dance numbers to songs from *Fiddler on the Roof.* Has anyone seen my eyeglasses?

Like that.

SPRING ARRIVED. Suburban gardens bloomed, plump dads pushed lawn mowers across the grass every Saturday. People played soccer in the park. My mother retiled our kitchen and my father joined a club for peo-ple interested in the history of the Civil War.

Demi and I watched *Cabaret* sixteen times. (Yes, we counted.) We spent a day talking only in sinister German accents. We bought fake noses at a theatrical and costume supply shop in Cleveland, glued them on with spirit gum, and wore them all day while we shopped in department stores. I directed *My Fair Lady: The Drag Interpretation* in Demi's living room while his parents were gone, to a wildly enthusiastic audience of no one. I played Henry Higgins, Colonel Pickering, Freddy Eynsford-Hill, and Alfred P. Doolittle, while Demi played Eliza and everyone else.

We saved each other, if you can call it saving when it takes the form of body glitter and cast albums and singing "Hot Lunch" in the back of a public bus.

And so, my life was no longer razzle-dazzle—deprived but utterly fabulous—as long as I was with Demi.

WE GOT our Wildewood acceptance letters on the same day.

I was in. He was in.

We were—we *were*—what we had hoped we were.

Good enough. Great.

Talented.

And—thank you, thank you, oh, Liza Minnelli and whatever other gods and goddesses watch over theater-mad, pizzazzy teenagers—we were *leaving Ohio*.

On June 24th, we packed our sheet music and our dance clothes, bought large amounts of potato products and sugary drinks, lost the map and then found it again, argued about what cast albums to bring for the road, dusted ourselves with body glitter, and got in my dad's beloved minivan to begin the endless drive to Wildewood.

Demi: Hold on, wait, oops--
(*thump, crash*)
Sadye: You're gonna break it!

Demi: No, I didn't. See? The
hoo-ji-whammer is still turning.

Sadye: Okay.

Demi: Okay then. *(deep breath)* Two
hours after our previous dispatch,
we would like to announce that
we can finally *see* it.

Sadye: We are going up a long
drive lined with trees.

Demi: *(disappointed)* It looks like
a boarding school.

Sadye: It *is* a boarding school. An
academy for the performing arts.
It goes all year.

Demi: Yeah, but didn't you think it
would look more--more theatrical?

Sadye: No.

Demi: It is way too preppy here.
We didn't drive six hours in
traffic to come to some prepston
boarding school.

Sadye: For posterity's sake, let
it be noted that Demi is having
a snit fit over architecture.
Probably because all he's eaten
today is potato chips, French
fries, and potato sticks.

Demi: Untrue. I had two Cokes

and one of your corn nuggy
things.

Sadye: Potato overdose always
makes you cranky.

Demi: For posterity, let it be
noted that Wildewood looks like
a collection of preppy brick
buildings and green lawns
nestled on the scenic edge of
Lake Ontario and--

Sadye: *(interrupting)* Ooh! There's
one of the theaters! The Kaufman
Theater, did you see?

Demi: Ooh! Okay, I'm happy now.
The theater looked big. That was
a honking big theater.

Sadye: Turn the recorder off.
We're here.

(thump, click)

WE PULLED UP in front of the dorms and parked.
Demi leaped out of the minivan and I followed; we did
a waggly joy dance as soon as our feet hit the pavement.

Then he disappeared.

It hadn't occurred to me that we wouldn't be
together until my father checked in with a counselor

and lugged Demi's suitcases over to one dormitory and mine to another. (Since Demi's parents had departed mid-June for a two-month second-honeymoon European tour/safari, my dad was in charge of both of us.)

Girls and boys.

Demi and I had slept on each other's shoulders on the bus to Cleveland. We had held hands in the movies and cried over the death of Tony in *West Side Story*. Once he even peed while I was in the shower at my house, pulling his hoodie down so it covered his eyes and barging through the door singing:

> *I'm not looking at you,*
> *no no no.*
> *You're not looking at me,*
> *no no no.*
> *I don't wanna see your*
> *scrawny girly booty.*
> *I just really*
> *really really*
> *hafta pee!*

We had always talked about going to Wildewood together. Everything, everything we did was together, everything—and now, there he was, walking into a red-brick building, popping back out to give his name to another, different clipboard person, getting his info packet, and disappearing again.

Gone.

My dad lugged my bags into my dormitory while I looked at a map of the campus and got my own info packet from a counselor.

"Do you want to come around with me and see the dance studios?" I asked, when my father returned. "They have five different theaters, too."

He looked at his watch.

"Come on, Dad," I pleaded. "You can take me to lunch and see what the cafeteria food's like."

"I want to beat the traffic home, Sarah. Your mother wants me to look at some tile this afternoon."

"But she's done with the floor."

"This is for the backsplash."

"You can't even walk around a bit, stretch your legs?"

He patted my shoulder. "I'd better be going." He gave me a kiss and got in the minivan.

THE DANCE studios were a cluster of rooms on the ground floor of an old stone building, with windows set high in the walls and doors open to the warm June air. There was no one around, so I went in.

The floors were scuffed, but the mirrors glowed and the pianos were baby grands—nothing like the battered uprights that had stood in the corners of Miss Delilah's rooms. I tapped a little, in my boots, then strolled down the hall to look at the girls' changing room. It had a large mirror outlined in lightbulbs and it stank with the familiar smell of sweat and shoe leather. I flipped a switch to turn the bulbs on and looked at myself in the glass; the too-bright light made me look older. I stared at my short, nearly black hair, the heavy eye makeup, the knee-high boots with bare legs, the purple suede mini, the glitter nail polish.

No one at Wildewood has ever met Sarah Paulson, I thought.

And none of them ever would. Here, I could be Sadye through and through. I could work my big nose, my gawky-sexiness, my height, my Broadway obsessions. Everything that made me out of place in Brenton would make me special here. I would let my Bigness out. Not just to Demi.

To the wide, wild world.

"Sadye, Sadye, Sadye," I whispered to the girl in the mirror. "Show me what you can do."

* * *

SOMEONE WAS playing piano in one of the studios.
"Big Spender." The song from *Sweet Charity*. It requires
horns—it's a hooting, bawdy number sung by a posse of
down-and-out girls who get paid to dance with men
at a seedy club—but the piano arrangement sounded
pretty good. I went down the hall and looked in.

A boy my age sat at the baby grand. He was Asian
American, medium weight, and looked to be about my
height. Shaggy black hair and a long oval face. A wide nose
that might have been broken once. Sharp eyes and a faded
blue T-shirt. He was looking down at the piano in complete
concentration. I could see his back muscles working
through the thin fabric. He had almost no hair on his arms.

I walked up to the piano and leaned over it, watching him play.

He didn't look up, but I could tell he knew I was
there. He was sweating slightly in the heat.

I'd never seen a guy my own age play the piano. It
was like sex and musical theater fused together.

A bead of moisture slid down his neck.

"I think *Charity* is one of the great underrated
musicals," I said, when "Big Spender" ended. "But I
don't know about that Christina Applegate version. I
like Shirley MacLaine better."

"They're all too old." The boy glanced up at me

but played a few chords from what I think was "Rich Man's Frug" with his right hand. "Gwen Verdon and Debbie Allen were too old, too."

"Did you see Christina? I only have the album."

"I live in Brooklyn," he said. "I go fairly often if I don't spend my money on pizza."

"How was she?"

"Good. She was good. But I think Charity should be played by someone in her early twenties."

"Isn't it more tragic if she's old?" I asked. "If she's been used so many times she can't count, and she still believes in love, still keeps hoping she can reinvent her rotten life?"

The boy considered. "Maybe. But maybe it's even sadder if she's been through all that and she's only twenty-one. And then the ending doesn't seem so self-delusional. Like maybe she *can* make a break."

"I always want to recast *The Music Man*," I said. "Because Marian the librarian is supposed to be this Balzac-reading rebel intellectual in this conservative town, and they always cast her as a wholesome Midwestern blonde. I think she should be homely."

He considered. "Good point. But I've got a soft spot for those Midwestern blondes."

I sighed. "All guys do, I think."

The boy laughed. His name was Theo. He went to

a private high school and played piano for all the school plays there. "I probably want to be a composer," he said. "For the stage. But last year I tried out and ended up being Sky Masterson in *Guys and Dolls* instead of staying in the orchestra, so I came to Wildewood to see if I've got what it takes."

"Me too." I said.

"All of us."

I asked him about New York City, and Theo told me about streets that were housing projects on one side and two-million dollar brownstones on the other. A block of nothing but Indian restaurants. A park designed for people to get lost in. Sunglasses for sale on the sidewalks, hundreds of colors, all selling cheap. He told me his parents didn't own a car. They ordered their groceries online and had them delivered. They took the subway. His mom was a law professor, his father a picture book artist.

I told him—well, there was nothing to say about Brenton. So I told him about Demi. How we did *Godspell Pillowcase* and *Sexy Fiddler* in my living room, with me serving as director and choreographer, Demi as costumer and scenic designer, playing all the parts ourselves, and my deaf and old parents barely even noticing.

Theo listened and laughed—but he only asked a question when I mentioned my mom's disability. "You mean you speak sign language?"

I shrugged. "Yeah."

"Amazing."

"I don't know about *that*."

"My parents always wanted me to learn Chinese, and I can speak a little, but I slagged off in Mandarin at Packer. I can't write it."

"Well, no one writes sign language."

"Still, you're bilingual."

"No, I'm not."

"You're fluent, aren't you?"

I am.

No one else, not even Demi, had ever put it that way. I am bilingual, I thought to myself. I am fluent in another language.

"I like watching people sign," Theo said, running his finger down the piano keys. "I guess it comes from playing piano. I'm interested in what people do with their hands."

"Play something else," I told him as I sat down on the piano bench.

And he did. He played songs from *Cabaret*, *West Side Story*, *Grease*, anything I asked for.

All from memory. All without missing a note.

I thought I might be in love.

* * *

MY DORM room was on the ground floor. It was larger than my bedroom at home, with dark wooden floors, an old radiator, two bunk beds, and windows looking across to the boys' dorm. Four cheap wooden dressers and a private bathroom with bare-bones fixtures. A sign on the inside of the door read: NO SINGING OR MUSICAL INSTRUMENT PRACTICE IS PERMITTED IN THE DORMITORIES BETWEEN 8 P.M. AND 8 A.M. THESE HOURS ARE FOR QUIET, REST, AND STUDY.

One of my three roommates, Isadora, was lying on a top bunk when I came in. "But call me Iz," she told me. "Everyone does."

She was wearing jean shorts and a bikini top. Her leg muscles were cut and her eyes were enormous. Strong jaw, pockmarked skin, curly brown hair.

I unzipped my duffel bag and started unpacking, stringing necklaces across the top of the mirror and hanging my sequined sweater off the end of the bunk bed for decoration, since it would probably be too hot to wear it much anyway. I had a poster from *Wicked* and another from the movie of *Cabaret* rolled in a cardboard tube. Iz lent me her tape.

Where was I from?

Ohio. Where was she from?

San Diego. Iz went to a specialized arts school

and studied voice and dance. Did I tap?

Yes. Did she?

Yes. Jazz?

Yes. Jazz?

Yes. Ballet?

Not really. Ballet?

Not really! What shows?

What?

What shows had I been in?

Oh. Um. A *West Side Story* medley at Miss Delilah's. What shows had she been in?

Damn Yankees, Kiss Me Kate, and *Born Yesterday,* last year at school. All leads.

Oh. Wow.

What were my electives?

Stage Combat and Restoration Comedy. What were hers?

Musical Theater Audition Prep and Restoration Comedy!

"I wanted M-TAP, but I didn't get it," I said.

"Everyone wants it," said Iz, stretching her feet up to touch the ceiling. "This is my third year here and I had to wait three years to get in. They're very selective."

I was about to ask her more, when a white-blond puff of pink looked in, nodded, waved as if to say, "Don't let me disturb you," disappeared, and then backed into the room, lugging an enormous duffel.

Iz and I fell silent while the girl, who was stout and sweating, climbed to the top of the second bunk, pulled a large *Jekyll & Hyde* poster out of the tube, and taped it up on the ceiling—presumably so she could look at it before she went to sleep.

Eeww.

I mean, it's one thing for me to have *Wicked* and *Cabaret* on the wall by the dressers, or for Iz to have Harry Connick, Jr. in *Pajama Game* up on one side of our bathroom door, and Hugh Jackman in *Oklahoma!* on the other—because those shows are all great. Hugh and Harry are both hot. But it is quite another thing to have a bizarre split-personality half-monster guy biting a prostitute. Which is what the *Jekyll & Hyde* poster was. I hadn't seen the musical, but I read the book in English, so I knew that Dr. Jekyll turns into a limping hunchback murderer whenever he drinks a magic potion, and that he is absolutely *not* the person you'd want staring down at you from above your bed.

"I'm Sadye," I said to the new girl, after she had finished taping. "And this is Isadora."

"Candie." Her pink tank top made her damp, flushed face appear even pinker, and she had the slightly hysterical look of a white toy poodle.

"Iz," I said. "Take a wild guess. What's our new roommate's favorite show?"

Isadora closed her eyes and pretended to think deeply. "Umm . . . *Jekyll & Hyde?*"

Candie nodded.

"I thought it closed ages ago," said Iz.

"In 2001. But I saw it, even though I was only eleven." Candie touched the poster gently. "It was my birthday present. Then I saw the tour, which was Chuck Wagner, you know, the guy who worked on it before Bob came on? He was amazing. I have all the different recordings."

I had no idea what she was talking about. She spoke as if this Bob guy were the president or Liza Minnelli or something.

"I saw Chuck do it twice. And last year I played Emma at school." Candie's face brightened. "We had to do extra performances; it was really popular."

"Nice," I said.

"I wanted to be Lucy, of course, everyone wants to be Lucy—that's the best part—but I was happy with Emma." Candie looked up at the creepy picture of the split-personality half-monster guy with love in her eyes. "My boyfriend played the lead. At least, he was my boyfriend during the show. Not that we're still together."

As we soon discovered, Candie's dominant characteristic was that she had no filter. She would lay out her whole life before total strangers. She was obsessed with the whole ex-boyfriend, *Jekyll & Hyde* experience, and had no ability whatsoever to think that maybe she'd want to present herself as seminormal to the people she'd be living with.

Foremost in her mind upon arriving at Wildewood was finding a good place for her Jekkie memorabilia—of which there were several other items now making their way out of her duffel—and she was unable to think of anything else until she'd finished setting them on her desk. Sheet music, several albums, *Playbill*s, a karaoke CD, the program from her high school production, and an autographed photo of "Bob" that she told us she had bought on eBay.

She was from New Jersey, exit number eight, ha-ha-ha, that's a New Jersey joke. She was the youngest child of five; her electives were M-TAP and Costume Design, her ex-boyfriend and she were meant to be and she knew he would come back around in the end because it was fate; she wanted to lose ten pounds—no, maybe fifteen; she hoped we'd all be best of friends; she was nervous about the dance classes; her mom took her into "the city" a month ago to see *Phantom of the Opera*; and what were we singing for the audition tomorrow?

Because she was singing "Memory" from *Cats* and she was so nervous she couldn't even see straight.

Truth was, Candie was acting exactly the way I *felt*. Thrilled, agitated, curious, a little stupid. But Candie was so wide open, her neediness was so real and sweaty—that my impulse was to pull away.

I was going to be Big at Wildewood. Not a gaping wound of need.

"I'm a mezzo belter," Iz was saying. "I'm never gonna get those high soprano leads so I don't even try. I'm doing 'Sandra Dee' from *Grease*."

"Oh, that's so great," said Candie. "I love that show. What are you doing, Sadye?"

"'Popular,'" I told her, applying eyeliner in the mirror. "From *Wicked*."

"You're a soprano, then?" she asked.

I didn't know.

What was I doing?

How could I not know?

"We did *Grease* and *West Side Story* here last year," said Iz, before I could answer. "And both times I was the feisty sidekick to the soprano lead. That's my luck. To be a sidekick forever."

"You played Anita?" I had entertained myself through many a boring math class by imagining myself as Anita in *West Side Story*.

"Yeah. I had a dress cut down to here—" Iz indicated a spot an inch or two above her navel.

"Va voom."

"But Rizzo was more fun, actually."

"Wait, you were here last year?" asked Candie.

Isadora nodded. "This is my third summer. The first year I was only fifteen, so I got little parts."

"Like what?" I asked, thinking, How bad does it get?

"I was an orphan in *Annie*—they made all the youngest kids be orphans 'cuz we were short—and I sang 'Turn Back, O Man' in *Godspell*."

"Oh, but that's good!" I blurted.

"It was okay," said Iz. "The second year was better."

"Why were you in two shows?" asked Candie. "I thought we were all in one."

"*Godspell* and *Grease* were ten-day wonders," answered Iz.

"Okay, stop everything," I declared. "What is a ten-day wonder?"

Iz walked me and Candie down through the green lawns and red-brick buildings to a small beach that bordered a lake at the south edge of campus, and explained how Wildewood functioned. Which was scary.

We'd have an orientation lecture that night, and

the next day a tour of the campus, free time to get to know each other, and a dance. "Then the craziness begins," said Iz. The next two days would be spent in public auditions, technically called Preliminary Songs and Monologues. We'd all go through a dance combination, then sit in the red velvet seats of the Kaufman Theater and watch each other do our sixteen-bar numbers and two-minute speeches. Jacob Morales was the head of the summer institute. He would give the lecture tonight and preside at the auditions—and (according to Iz) he was brilliant. A Broadway director, fresh off the smash of last season's *Oliver!* revival.

(At this, I wanted to squeal, though I managed to hold it in. *Oliver! Oliver!* that Demi and I had been listening to all morning! Why hadn't it occurred to me to Google the institute faculty?)

Iz had had Morales for acting class two years in a row, and he'd directed her in *Godspell* and *Grease*. "He always does the ten-day wonder," she said. "That's why it's good to get cast in it. I learned so much from him."

"Like what?" I asked.

She didn't answer. By now we were taking off our shoes to walk in the sand, and she bent down to unbuckle her sandals. "The ten-day wonder is because they want to get people out in front of an audience," she explained. "The directors want us to have a play of our own right away, before any of the other shows are ready. To get us into the spirit of performance."

"Okay."

"After the auditions, everyone's in a show. And your show rehearses in the afternoon. But some people are in the ten-day wonder also, and then you have rehearsals at night and don't go to evening rec. You even get out of classes some mornings, because you're putting up this show as fast as you can." Iz smiled happily. "It's so, so stressful."

"That's how you did *Grease*?" Candie dipped one curvy toe into the icy lake water. Her feet were cute and decorated with sparkly white polish. Dancers never have cute feet.

"And *Godspell*," said Iz. "The night after the auditions, Morales and the other directors all meet and argue over casting. They stay up all night—because in the morning, before breakfast, they have to post a cast list for every show."

There were four musicals, she explained, plus the ten-day wonder, plus a classic straight play, usually Shakespeare. "But you don't want to be in the straight play," she said. "Trust me. It's like the catchall for people with no talent."

Candie moaned. "If they put me in *Hamlet* I'll die."

"Wait. Did you hear they're doing *Hamlet?*" Iz asked, looking intent.

Candie shrugged. "How would I know? I meant I don't want to talk Shakespeare," said Candie. "I can never understand what they're saying."

"You have to be able to do Shakespeare if you're going to be an actress," I said.

"Say *actor*," corrected Iz. "That's what they say here. Boy. Girl. Everyone's an actor."

"Shakespeare's the greatest dramatist ever," I told Candie. "You can't be scared of him or you'll never make it."

Candie shook her frizzy curls. "I just want to do a show with music. I wish I could dance."

"Well," I said. "Do you take classes?"

"No."

"You don't take dance classes?"

"I said no."

"Then you haven't tried. You have to study it for years before you can seriously complain that you can't dance. Otherwise you're making excuses."

I was being awful to Candie, I knew. Condescending. Something in Candie's naked fear and strange obsessions—something in her awkward, apple-shaped body—made me afraid.

Afraid of being lumped in with her.

I knew I could dance. And yet I also felt like Candie did: I didn't know if I'd be good enough. And I hated the way Iz had corrected me—"Say *actor*, that's what they say here." Reminding me how little I knew. And it was so, so irritating how Iz's definition of a bad part was one I'd kill to have ("Turn Back, O Man") and how she was completely confident of her own worth. "Everyone knows me here," she said at one point. "You don't play Anita and Rizzo in one year and not have the teachers know you."

I don't mean to make it sound like Iz was horrible. She wasn't. It was more like she was bursting with stories and tips and excitement, and it was all spilling out of her, the way she knew so much and had been in so many shows. She was helping us, really. She was being generous, but at the same time every sentence she spoke reminded us that she was a long-time veteran, sure of hefty parts in two showy musicals, while we were scared newbies who didn't even know what a ten-day wonder was until she explained it to us.

There on the beach, what Iz was really telling me and Candie was that she was so good, and so experienced, there was no way we could ever compete with her. And I was telling Candie she hadn't worked as hard as I had and didn't have the drive she needed. And

Candie was still oblivious to the status game, letting all her insecurities hang out.

Yes, I was mean to Candie.

Yes, I would have been nicer person if I had opted out of the competition and just let Iz ramble on about how talented she was. But that's not what I did.

I hadn't come to Wildewood to back down at the first sign of a challenge. I had come to show what I could do, right? To let the Bigness out.

I stood on my hands in the sand and split my legs in the air. A perfect 180-degree split into a front walkover.

Then I did it again.

It shut Iz up.

But only temporarily.

OUR FOURTH roommate was brushing her hair when we returned to get ready for dinner. Her name was Nanette, and she was a strawberry blonde with a pointy chin and a body so small you'd have thought she was twelve. We hadn't even reached the cafeteria before we learned that Nanette had played Chip in *Beauty and the Beast* on Broadway when she was seven, followed by a touring production of *Annie* in which she understudied the lead. She then played Jemima in *Chitty Chitty Bang Bang*, back on Broadway, did a revival of *A Little Night Music* in Los Angeles, and since then had been traveling the West Coast in a nine-month tour of *Fiddler on the Roof*. Although she was sixteen, she was so tiny she played the youngest of Tevye's daughters.

"I'm here to rest," she said. "I need time off to not be working, you know? But I'd miss the theater too much if I did anything this summer besides come here."

"Do you go to school?" I asked as we took our trays into the cafeteria and sat down.

"Professional Children's."

"What's that?"

"You never heard of it?"

"No."

"The Professional Children's School in New York. It's for kids who work in the arts; they e-mail your homework to you and stuff, so you can keep up while you're on tour."

"Oh."

"I've barely set foot in the place for like the past two years. It's all been fax and e-mail. They give you a laptop."

"Does your mom or dad go with you? On tour?"

"My dad used to. I have two sisters and a brother, so my mom couldn't. But when I got *Night Music*, my younger sister Kylie had started getting commercials, so my dad had to stay home to manage her audition schedule. And my brother is on a soap, so my dad helps with that, too. But don't worry"—Nanette laughed at my surprised face—"I had a host family to stay with. And on *Fiddler* my stage manager looked out for me. She's the best. It's like we're sisters." Nanette took a bite of a soggy-looking taco and put it down. "Do you have a boyfriend?"

I was startled by her change of topic, but I shook my head. "Boys in my hometown like the plain vanilla," I said. "I think I'm more mint chocolate chip."

"Ha!" Nanette barked her laugh. "Love it. This vanilla thing is causing you serious lack-of-boyfriend issues, then?"

I nodded. "I'm hoping to improve the situation this summer."

"Mint chocolate chip is a good flavor. It's sophisticated. And it's green, which is unusual. I think I'm more of a . . . let me see. Toffee. Is that a flavor? Looks like vanilla but has crunchy bits mixed in. Almost a burned flavor."

"What am I?" asked Candie.

Nanette looked at her appraisingly. "Let's see. Do *you* have a boyfriend?"

"I used to." Candie twirled a curl around her index finger. "But not anymore. I don't think."

"You don't know?"

"He's not my boyfriend anymore," Candie said. "But he was for a while."

"I think maybe you're strawberry," I offered.

"Why?"

"You wear pink. You're like pink and white."

Candie wrinkled her nose. "I don't want to be strawberry," she said. "I want to be something else."

"I'm chocolate with chocolate fudge ripples," announced Iz. "And before you ask, yes I do have a boyfriend."

We all perked up, and Iz told us about her motorcycle-riding, already graduated boyfriend named Wolf, who was waiting for her all summer while she was away; who she'd been to third base with but not the full shebang; who worked in a record store and loved *Avenue Q* and Coldplay, both. "He knows everything about music," she told us. "And when I graduate, we're forming a band and I'm going to be lead singer."

"Do you have a boyfriend, Nanette?" I wanted to know. Since she started the conversation.

She shook her head. "There were no guys my age in *Fiddler*. I haven't even been around any decent boys for like years. It's a hazard of my profession." She looked around the cafeteria. "Half these guys are gay, I bet."

"Yeah," I said. "But you know what? The other half aren't."

"And maybe they like mint chocolate chip." Nanette smiled.

"Or toffee."

"Nobody likes strawberry," moaned Candie. "Strawberry is a kid flavor."

I felt bad about how mean I'd been to her earlier, on the beach. "You don't have to be strawberry. You can be cherries jubilee."

Candie smiled. "Okay, that's good. Cherries jubilee."

Iz stood up. "Speaking of—"

"What?"

"Hetero boys," she said. "That guy over there is exactly a mint-chocolate-chip type of guy. I'm gonna go talk to him, see if I can get him to come by our room later to um . . . have a taste."

"Gross!" yelled Nanette. "We have to stop this game now, if that's where it's leading."

"Which one?" I wanted to know.

"The one in the green hoodie."

I looked over at him. He was tall, with a round face and a big smile. Braces on his teeth. Rings on his fingers. Hair spiked up with gel.

"He played Kenickie in *Grease*," said Iz, as if that

was all I needed to know. "So I've already kissed him and can tell you, he's good. His name is James."

She bused her tray and crossed the cafeteria, calling out, "Greased Lightnin'!" at the top of her lungs.

Nanette ate a French fry and changed the subject. "I heard they were doing *Bye Bye Birdie* and *Little Shop of Horrors* this year."

We leaned in close. "How do you know?" breathed Candie. "You just got here."

"My agent knows Jake." Nanette shrugged. "She called him and asked—and that's what he told her."

"Who's Jake?"

"Jake Morales? Only the director of the program."

"Oh, right."

"We're doing *Midsummer*, too, because they always have to do one straight play, something classical," said Nanette.

"*A Midsummer Night's Dream?*" said Candie, her pink face going pale at the thought of Shakespeare.

"Hello? What other *Midsummer* is there?"

Candie looked down and took a bite of fruit salad.

"What else?" I asked. "Aren't there five shows? Wait, no, five plus the ten-day wonder is six."

"Ten-day wonder?"

Aha. Nanette didn't know about the ten-day wonder, and Candie and I gleefully informed her, like we were old-timers.

"Jake said *Birdie, Midsummer, Little Shop, Show Boat, Guys and Dolls,* and . . . oh. *Cats,*" Nanette went on, counting shows on her fingers.

"*Cats!*" squealed Candie. "I love *Cats!*"

"Sweet pea," said Nanette. "Keep your voice down. You are *not* supposed to love *Cats.*"

Iz had arrived back at our table. "Oh, no, not *Cats!*"

"Yes," said Nanette, her voice animated with faux dread. "*Cats.*"

"I saw it at the Winter Garden before it closed," said Candie. "It was so amazing. Why don't you like it?"

Okay. In case you haven't heard of *Cats*—because it closed ages ago and Candie must have seen it when she was little—it was the longest running Broadway show *ever,* and involves people dressed up as kitty cats, dancing in feline fashion. There is one sad, aging alley cat who dies and goes to cat heaven, but the rest are happy and leap around singing about themselves.

Cats is one of those shows that everyone thought was great when it came out, because it was based on these T. S. Eliot poems that are actually pretty funny and he's like a famous poet. Then it became this hackneyed tourist trap that people would come to see because it was a famous spectacle, but not because it was art.

Even Demi and I, in the depths of Ohio, had figured out that it was embarrassing to like *Cats*. But Candie loved it.

"Never mind," said Nanette dismissively, and filled Iz in on the shows for that year.

THEO WAS standing near the exit when I left the cafeteria, talking with a group of Wilders (that's what we were called). He'd changed his T-shirt, and his thick hair was still damp from the shower.

I was nervous, and part of me wanted to walk on with my roommates and not go after him, but then I thought—no. I'm here to try and get things I want. And that piano-playing boy is one of those things.

I should do something. Fall on my face if I have to.

"Theo," I called, and he turned around. "Walk me to the dorm and I'll tell you secrets."

It worked. He ran over and jostled my shoulder playfully. "That's a small price to pay, if the secrets are any good."

"They're good. I promise you."

I wanted to touch him, so I put my hand on the back of his neck and whispered in his ear. "*Show Boat. Cats. Midsummer Night's Dream. Bye Bye Birdie. Little Shop of Horrors.* Oh, and . . . *Guys and Dolls.*"

"You know for sure?" he asked.

I shook my head. "But one of my roommates has an inside line."

"That's my show," he said as we walked down the path toward the dormitories. "That's my show and that's my part. Sky Masterson."

"I know it."

"You tell a good secret, Sadye," said Theo. "You got any more like that?"

"Maybe," I answered. "Let me see how good you are at walking me places first."

"Oh, I'm fantastic at walking you places. Can't you tell? Look at me, putting one foot in front of the other as if I've been doing it all my life."

I laughed.

"You'll see," Theo went on. "I'll walk you straight to your door. I may even come in for a moment, if that'll get me extra secrets."

He wanted to come in! Forget James/Kenickie. Theo the piano man was coming to my dorm room! "You'll have to beware the *Jekyll & Hyde* poster," I warned him. "It's seriously disturbing."

"Oh, I've survived worse already today," he said. "One of my roommates put up a giant picture of Andrew Lloyd Webber."

We were strolling past the boys' dormitory when I spotted Demi sitting on the steps, eating a bag of peanut M&M's—and glowing. "Sadye!" he yelled, jumping up and pulling me into a bear hug. "Oh, my darling, do I have stuff to tell you!"

"What's up? Why weren't you at dinner?"

"I have stuff to tell you!"

"I heard. Demi, this is Theo. Theo, Demi. My friend from home."

"Hi, hi, nice to meet you," Demi said, waving. "But I have to steal Sadye now. I'm sorry, it's a drama, it's like stuff is happening in my life and I need that Sadye consult!"

"Oh. Um. Okay." Theo shrugged.

"Okay, bye!"

"Sorry!" I called as Demi grabbed my arm and yanked me into the boys' dorm, leaving Theo out on the quad.

"S'okay!" he called back.

"Wait!" I said to Demi as soon as we were out of earshot. "Tell me what you think. Is he cute, or what?"

"Very cute. A little short for you."

"I think he might like me. We met in the dance studio."

"Later, all right?"

"He was walking me to my dorm. You dragged me away! At least let me dish!"

"But this is important!"

"Hey, I know what shows we're doing."

"Come back to my room so I can tell you. Why are you lollygagging? Oh, wait." Demi was halfway down the hall, dragging me by the hand. "What?"

"I know what shows we're doing."

"What are they?"

"No, tell me your stuff. Now that you dragged me away."

"No, tell me the shows!"

"No, now I want to know the stuff!"

We went into his room, which was identical to mine, except sadly undecorated. (Boys.)

"I kissed someone." Demi wiggled around in excitement.

"What?"

"I did already. The guy down the hall!"

"You did not."

"I did. Blake from Boston. Blond Blake from Boston."

Not only had Demi never had a boyfriend, I

honestly don't think he had ever kissed anybody before—though I wasn't sure. A guy with his ego would never admit to seventeen and never-been-kissed. But Demi had been a picked-on, beat-up underclassman in Detroit—and so invisible he never had an opportunity in Brenton. At least, not an opportunity that he could find.

"How did it happen?" I asked.

"Everyone went to dinner, but I felt gross so I wanted to take a shower, and when I got out, Blake poked his head in the door and said his name, and asked did I know where the cafeteria was."

"Were you naked?"

"What? No! What kind of boy do you think I am?"

"From the shower."

"No, I had already gotten dressed."

"Okay, so Blake comes in and asks you where the cafeteria is, and . . ."

"And he comes in, and we were chatting, la la la, about whatever, how he was in *Oklahoma!* at school this spring, and I was sitting on my bottom bunk and he just came and sat next to me, and the next I knew, he kissed me!"

"That's so European."

"I *know*."

"A blond boy came in and made out with you for no reason."

"Yes!"

"And that's why you missed dinner?"

"Yes!"

"Are you going to go out with him?"

"I have no idea!" Demi seemed unconcerned. He was so immersed in the idea that he'd had a kissing adventure.

"Wait, I have to see him!" I jumped up and headed for the door.

"No, you can't!" Demi grabbed my arm, laughing. "You can't go looking, he'll know I sent you!"

"No, he won't. He'll think I'm some random girl."

"Sadye, I can't believe you! Don't! Okay, be subtle," he yelled as I wrenched my hand out of his and opened the door. "Oh, no! Wait!" Demi called after me down the hall. "Back up! It's the other way!"

I reversed direction and walked until I saw a door with the name Blake on it. I knocked and pushed my head in. A semispherical white boy with black-rimmed glasses, wearing a checked shirt and vintage pants, was reading on one of the beds. "I'm looking for Blake," I said.

"Isn't everybody?" he said, his voice nasal.

"Is everybody?"

"He's kind of a god," said the boy. Then he waved a funny little wave as if to say that he, too, appreciated the sexual appeal of Blond Blake from Boston. "I'm Lyle. Who are you?"

"Sadye."

"Blake is not floating in your direction, Sadye, if you know what I mean."

"Oh, I know. I know." I dropped my voice to a whisper. "I just wanted to get a look at him. Like a reconnaissance mission for a friend."

Lyle nodded.

"I love your pants," I said. And I did. They were sharkskin, dusky blue with a silvery shine.

"Thanks," he said. And actually blushed. Like girls didn't give him compliments often. "You'll see Blake at the Meat Market, day after tomorrow, anyway. Everyone will," he told me.

"The Meat Market?"

"Auditions. You know, we all sit and watch each other."

"Aha."

"Aha, indeed. You check out the talent, sure— but there's not much you can do about that. Morales is going to pick who he picks, and the rest will get the leftovers, and that's that. So what auditions are for is— romance."

Lyle spoke like an observer, not like a participant. He was plump and a bit hairy for someone our age, and he wore those black-rimmed glasses and vintage clothes with such an aggressive awkwardness it was geektastic.

"How come you're such an expert?" I asked.

"I go to Wildewood year-round," he said. "And this is my second summer. I went through this whole melodrama last year."

I plunked myself on Blond Blake's bed. Lyle was chatty. He told me how last year, Iz had stepped into the part of Anita when the girl playing it was caught sneaking off campus for the third time and got sent home, and before that she had only been in the chorus. How Blond Blake from Boston did push-ups in the middle of the dorm room here on the first day, as if he couldn't skip a single twenty-four-hour period of bod-buffing. How he (Lyle) had been Smee in *Peter Pan* last summer, and the guy playing Captain Hook had to wear tight red latex pants, but no one had thought to explain to him the proper underclothing. How he (Lyle again) was from a small town in Vermont and his mom was a boozer, so he was glad to be sent to boarding school because "sometimes it got ugly in the evenings." How he'd gotten into Wildewood by doing Richard III for his monologue at the age of thirteen. He'd read Royal Shakespeare Company star Antony Sher's book about playing the part and cribbed all the details of

Sher's performance (as he imagined them) for his audition.

I asked him about going to Wildewood full time, and he said it was more boarding schoolish: do your homework, be on a sports team, lots of people studying classical music, classes in theater history, scene study in Ibsen and Chekhov. "For the summer institute, Morales takes over," he explained. "You know he directed the revival of *Oliver!* that's on Broadway now?"

I nodded.

"It was amazing. A group of us took the bus in to see it. Anyway, with him in charge, Wildewood's all about show biz." Lyle flashed jazz hands at me. "The straight play is just a requirement the school insists on to keep the classical training rep."

He was a great raconteur, Lyle. Full of Lurking Bigness.

It was like that at Wildewood—nearly everyone I met, no matter how ordinary or subordinary their physical appearance, seemed to have that light inside them. Lyle walking down the street would be practically invisible. But Lyle talking—waving his hands and doing funny voices—I couldn't look away.

Lyle, Theo, Isadora, Nanette—all of them were huge personalities. Personae, even. The way Demi was. Convinced of their own fabulousness and eager to show it to the world.

And if they weren't like that, they were like Candie. People whose inner lives flashed across their faces with startling transparency, whose hunger was so strong you could feel it when you looked at them, and it made you want to look away. There were quite a few of these raw types at Wildewood, though not nearly so many as there were the fabulositons. The raw types were the ones who got beat up in high school. Who felt like there was no one at home who understood how they felt. The ones who escaped into theater, hoping it would save them from themselves—and sometimes it did.

When people like Candie came to the summer institute, even if they weren't popular, even if they weren't beautiful, even if they couldn't dance, even if they got a lame part in an even lamer show—they felt like they'd come home. Because it was a world where they could live and breathe theater, and they wanted nothing else so badly as they wanted that.

Now that I think of it, maybe Demi was more like them than I knew.

I'D BEEN talking with Lyle for forty-five minutes when Demi poked his head into the room, looking for me. I had so forgotten my reconnaissance mission that I was surprised to see him.

"Miss Sadye," he scolded, swishing in wearing his favorite silver shirt and brown leather pants, glitter splashed across his cheekbones, "are you going to orientation in that tired old skirt? Because I know you can do better."

Orientation started in ten minutes in the Kaufman Theater.

"Lyle, meet my friend Demi, from home," I said. "Demi, meet Lyle: genuine full-time student at Wildewood, Shakespearean heavy-hitter, former sidekick to Captain James Hook, and wearer of excellent pants."

"Hey," said Demi.

"Hey," said Lyle.

And I could tell. From the way Lyle looked down at his hands after they were introduced. From the way he snuck another look at Demi in his most flamboyant mode, dragging me up off the floor and tsk-tsking at the low quality of my outfit. Lyle said, "Sadye, why don't you go change, and Demi and I will come pick you up outside your dorm in five minutes?"—and anyone could tell.

I could. Demi could.

Lyle had a crush.

* * *

FOR ORIENTATION, we assembled in the Kaufman Theater. Lyle, Nanette, Demi, and I arrived early and got seats middle center. We put our feet on the chairs in front of us and watched the parade of Wilders come into the space.

By and large, people were dramatic. Ridiculous, even. Thrift store dresses and too much makeup, ballet shoes with street clothes, hair streaked blue or pink. Eighties throwback shirts with the necks cut out; riots of color. But one thing was like Brenton: nearly everyone was white. There were maybe six African American girls and only three guys, one being Demi. Then maybe four other people of color, including Theo, who sat way down front and seemed like he didn't see me.

"Point out Blake," I whispered.

"I can't see him."

"He must be here somewhere."

Demi swiveled. "Way in the back, there. Don't look! Don't look. Okay, now!"

Blake turned out to be tall, with male good looks, like he was carved out of rock: cleft chin, corn-silk hair, muscles. Not my type at all, but I said "Ooh la la" anyway.

Demi giggled. "I know! Stop looking, stop looking! He's going to see us!"

I turned back around.

"Don't look at him again! I am being nonchalant," Demi whispered, surveying the room, which was now nearly full. "Oh, baby. If those other black boys can't sing, I'm gonna be stuck with 'Ol' Man River.'"

("Ol' Man River," in case you don't already know, is a famous number from *Show Boat*; it's a big, slow song for a black man with a large, deep voice, where he symbolizes the American South in a philosophical and somewhat hokey but also beautiful way.)

"That wouldn't be too bad," I said, though I was thinking Demi's voice wasn't low enough for "Ol' Man River."

"No way," said Demi. "I don't want to play some old symbolic guy. There is way too much sex appeal in this body to be stuck Ol' Man Rivering just because I am the right color."

"Maybe they have color-blind casting."

"Maybe. But I doubt it. Not for 'Ol' Man River,' anyway."

I didn't want to get too deep into the race issue just then. Honestly, I never did. Demi and I had talked about it before, but whenever it came up—his blackness, my whiteness—we were talking about the only thing that separated us.

Most of the time we felt the same. We *were* the

same. We were together. Boy/girl, gay/straight—those divisions were invisible to us, because we were the geek-tastic drama queens of Brenton, destined for Broadway—and that was what mattered.

But when the black/white difference came up, as it did every now and again, I could feel a break between us. Like there was something about me that he'd never understand all the way, and something about him that I wouldn't either.

And when I felt separate from Demi, I felt lost. So I didn't want to go there. "Let's talk about me," I said with exaggerated drama. "Let's think of some lead parts for tall skinny flat-chested girls with big noses!"

"*Funny Girl,*" Demi answered off the bat. "And maybe *Victor/Victoria.*"

"You're good," said Nanette, who had been quiet up to this point. "How about for girls under five feet tall? I'm such a shrimp, I'll be playing children forever."

Oh, so irritating. And a perfect example of what everyone was always doing at Wildewood. Because when Nanette said, "I'll be playing children forever," though superficially she was self-deprecating, she was also reminding us of her vast professional experience playing kids, and her assurance that she had a long career in front of her. And, as if to prove me right, this was what she said next: "They're reviving *The Secret*

Garden at La Jolla Playhouse next fall, then maybe moving it to Broadway. I have an audition in a couple weeks."

"Where?"

"The theater's near San Diego but the audition's in L.A. The director goes up to L.A. and sees actors from all over."

"You're flying cross-country for an audition?"

"My dad thinks I should go. I guess the director saw me in *Night Music* and wanted to call me in."

Demi sighed, and I knew he felt like I did: Nanette already had what we both wanted. She'd had it for years.

"Don't say shrimp," I told her. "Say Kristinish. Kristin has opened up doors for shrimpy women everywhere. You could play anything."

There was a tap on the microphone stage left. We settled into silence. There behind a podium stood a white woman with prominent teeth, fluffy gray-blond hair, and a dress of indistinct shape. She informed us that we should settle down now, and welcomed the group to Wildewood's Summer Institute. Her name was Reanne Schuster. "I'll be teaching Acting and the Classical Monologue elective," she announced. "And I'll direct an ensemble production of *A Midsummer Night's Dream* by William Shakespeare."

A ripple went through the crowd. Rumors had been flying about what shows we'd be performing, but this was the first formal announcement. Nanette tipped her head at me as if to say "See? My information comes from the top."

"And now, without further ado," said Reanne, "I present you with the Summer Institute's artistic director: the inimitable, the wonderful, the Tony-winning— Jacob Morales."

We clapped, and I was a bit surprised to see the disheveled man from the auditions—the one with the beard who had snorted at my Juliet—mount the stairs and take the microphone in his hand.

Morales wore a wrinkled white shirt, baseball cap, khaki shorts, and sandals. I could see the shine on his forehead, and his ankles looked thick and unhappy, somehow. "Welcome," he said in his thin, high voice. "We are all here to create. Yes? To make something out of nothing. This summer, you will be bringing words on the page into vivid life. You will turn scatterings of musical notes into songs full of expression and meaning. You will also work harder than you've ever worked before."

He ran a hand through his thinning hair. "When I was directing *Oliver!* this past fall," (shouts and whistles from a few in the audience) "many members of the cast were younger than you are. My star was only eleven, and he carried a Broadway show every night."

Nanette, on my right, whispered: "They have two kids doing that part on alternate performances. I know it for a fact. Nobody that age can sustain an eight-show schedule with a five-show weekend."

Morales went on: "I watched you audition myself, in cities across the country. I saw each and every one of you perform, and so I know I'm right when I tell you that you, too, have the talent it takes to do that. To carry a show. There is terrific talent in this room. Star-level talent."

Another cheer.

"However, your talent may be buried, or it may be undeveloped. It may be clouded by ego and the desire to show the world what you can do. Here at the Wildewood Summer Institute, we help you develop your physical instrument: the voice, the breath, the body. We give you techniques for both self-expression and transformation. And then we bring it all together and put on some of the greatest shows anywhere."

More cheering.

Morales gestured for Reanne (in the front row) to bring him her bottle of water, which she did. "However," he said, after taking a long drink, "you must remember that an essential aspect of an actor's craft is humility. And the eradication of the ego for the good of the show will be an essential part of our philosophy here.

"I mean this in two ways. First of all, to truly embody a character, to truly *act*, involves releasing yourself from the mannerisms, tics, fears, and foibles that are part of your own character. To become someone else, you must let go of yourself, and to do that, you must be humble.

"It is also true that not everyone can be a star. Not in a single summer with only six productions. You may not love the part you get. You may not even like it. You may think you should have a lead, or a chance to shine in a different way. But what you must do, what you *must do* if you are committed to the craft of the theater, is to release yourself from those complaints and join together with your fellow cast members to make the show you are in the best show it can be.

"When you leave the room tonight, I want you to take a stone from the dish in the lobby. We have one for each and every one of you, and I want you to treasure that stone this summer, and come back to it when your sense of ego, when your sense of your own importance, is getting in the way of creating good theater.

"Theater is a collective effort, a community endeavor. I am pleased to be going on this journey with you," he said. "And I look forward to another spectacular summer."

The students erupted in applause as Morales made his way back to his seat.

"He's amazing," I whispered to Demi. "I hope I get him for acting."

Demi nodded. "*Oliver!* got phenomenal reviews. I can't believe we're here."

"Me either."

He squeezed my hand. "You'll see. We'll take this place *over*."

"What happened to 'eradicate your ego'?"

"Oops! I already forgot." Demi giggled.

"Maybe he meant confidence and ego are different," I whispered. "Like you need the confidence, but you have to leave the ego behind?"

"He's the man, that's all I'm gonna say. Whatever that guy wants, that is what I'll do."

From the front row, a tall, narrow woman—obviously a dancer—with a shock of pink hair rose to take the stage. "I'm Tamar," she announced, "and I'll be choreographing two of the shows and teaching advanced dance classes. I'm here to announce the productions we'll be doing this year."

A murmur ran through the audience. "That's his girlfriend," whispered Nanette.

"Whose?"

"Jake's."

Jacob Morales.

"My agent told me his girlfriend was a choreographer with pink hair."

It was less hard to believe than it had been before I'd heard him speak. Morales was physically unattractive and had a strange voice—but he had charisma.

Tamar announced the shows. They were just as Nanette had told us they would be:

A Midsummer Night's Dream

Bye Bye Birdie

Show Boat

Little Shop of Horrors

Cats

and *Guys and Dolls* (the ten-day wonder).

WE ALL TOOK stones from the bowl on our way out. Mine was smooth and hard and black. Demi's was pinkish with white flecks. I put mine on my dresser at curfew, or at least I think I did. But in the morning, I couldn't find it.

* * *

THE NEXT day, we assembled for a three-hour tour of the campus. Lyle, Candie, and Demi were in my group—but of course Lyle didn't need the tour at all, having lived at Wildewood for the past three years. So he entertained us by muttering addendums to the information we were being given. The lakefront beach was, according to Lyle, "the site of several midnight debaucheries resulting in expulsion," and the boys' dorm had the "second best roof on campus, each roof receiving points for comfort, view, ease of access, and privacy."

There were five theaters (one outdoors—which would be for *Show Boat*), and their lobby walls were lined with photographs of past student productions. We strolled across brilliant green lawns to dance studios and rehearsal rooms, and poked our heads into the Performing Arts Library, which included videotapes of famous productions, scrapbooks on theater programs, and hundreds of books on theater and dance history.

Basements of the dorms and classrooms contained practice rooms with pianos and soundproof walls ("You don't even want to *know* what goes on down there late nights," muttered Lyle), and the math and science buildings were small and neglected in comparison with the performing arts centers. We saw the costume studio, filled with racks of sparkly clothes and bolts of fabric, the walls covered with design sketches of elongated figures. We took the freight elevator to the lumber shop, where flats from sets for *A Doll's House* and *Arcadia* (two spring shows at the Academy) were leaned up against each other, a cacophony of floral wallpapers.

"We don't have anything like this in New Jersey," Candie whispered. "I mean, my high school has like, an auditorium and that's it."

I knew what she meant, but I didn't want to sound ignorant. "There are lots of programs like this," I told her. "Interlochen, Stagedoor Manor." I had looked them up on the Internet.

"I know," said Candie. "I just didn't know how big it would be; how different it would feel to actually stand here and be a part of it all."

"Don't be fooled by tour-guide patter," said Lyle, coming up behind us. "It's not all spotlights and glamour."

"Oh, I know we've got to work hard," said Candie. "Morales told us."

"That's not what I meant," Lyle told her. "I meant that this place can be hard as hell to take. There's a lot of blood spilled in the creation of musical comedy. You'd be surprised."

"Don't you love it?" I asked.

"Of course I do. It's my home," Lyle said. "But I'm not afraid to tell you: it's dysfunctional."

"You don't know from dysfunctional, darling," Demi butted in. "This place is heaven."

At LUNCHTIME, the tour finished in front of the cafeteria. "Do you see Blake?" Demi asked, looking around.

"No, I don't, happy to say," muttered Lyle.

"Blake is that cute blond guy, right?" Candie said to me. "Don't you think he's cute?"

"Certainly, darling," I said. "But forget it."

Candie looked crushed. "I didn't mean he'd ever look at me," she said, louder. "Gosh, Sadye. I know I'm not—"

"Don't be so mean, Sadye. You're giving the girl a complex," interrupted Demi, putting his arm around Candie.

"I was explaining the Blake situation," I told him.

"Sadye didn't mean it how it sounded," Demi said to Candie. "Whatever horrible thing she said."

"I didn't," I told Candie. "Really." And that was true.

But it was also true that I hated her neediness, her naked, naked feelings.

"Blake is . . . European," joked Demi.

"What do you mean, European?" asked Candie, confused.

"Here's the deal," Demi explained kindly. "Blond Blake from Boston belongs to me."

Candie laughed. "What, like you're gay?" She said it as if it could only be a joke.

Demi looked at her, his face harsher. "Exactly."

Candie looked abashed. "Oh, my gosh."

"Don't be shocked," said Lyle. "This is musical theater."

Candie was from a Christian family, I knew. Her parents were conservative. I bet she'd never seen an out gay person in her life. "I never would have thought . . ." she stuttered. "Blake is so . . ."

"Isn't he, though?" sighed Demi. "So so so so . . ."

"Welcome to Wildewood, Candie," said Lyle nasally. "I think you're going to have a very interesting summer."

As soon as we spotted Blake in the cafeteria (in line at the salad bar), Demi was gone. And Lyle ran after Demi.

Candie and I found seats with Iz and Nanette. We

ate grilled cheese with coleslaw on the side and claimed parts for ourselves in the big musicals. Iz, the mezzo, wanted Miss Adelaide in *Guys and Dolls* and Rose in *Bye Bye Birdie*, both fiery characters who get their reluctant guys to the altar by the end of the show. Nanette, also a belter, but more of a leading lady type, wanted Audrey in *Little Shop*—a buxom, vulnerable blonde with the brainpower of a pea and a heart as big as Texas. She said she'd also be happy with Julie in *Show Boat*. "But you know me," she said, (although we didn't), "I'll get stuck with the little brother in *Birdie*. Because of my size. The curse of the tiny."

Candie hoped meekly to sing a solo. When pressed, she said she'd be glad to get Grizabella in *Cats*.

"What do you want, Sadye?" Iz asked me.

I was terrified I'd end up a dancer in the background of *Cats* without ever speaking or singing a word onstage all summer. And I already felt sick at the supposedly friendly competition between us all, which (if it went on like this) might mean that none of us would ever be friends, no matter if we ate every meal together for seven weeks. No way would I land a high soprano part like Kim in *Birdie* or Magnolia in *Show Boat*. I didn't have the vocal power for *Little Shop*, either. Rose in *Birdie* was a possibility, but my best bet was the shrieky Brooklynette babe, Miss Adelaide, who shakes her tail feathers in *Guys and Dolls* as a featured act at the Hot Box club.

So I replied to Iz's question with an answer she didn't want to hear: "Adelaide."

Iz looked at me for a moment without saying a word. Then she stood up and climbed onto her chair. Standing with one foot on the table next to her grilled cheese, hip cocked out, hands fluttering around her face in comical confusion, she began to sing. "Take Back Your Mink"—Adelaide's big number.

The cafeteria hushed. Isadora's slightly gritty belt soared—all about a fur coat, a beautiful gown, and the no-good fella who bought them for her and then figured he'd bought himself the chance to undress her.

The song sounded good, a capella. Her voice was a jazz trumpet. It announced itself, bossy and smoky at the same time, piercing at the high notes and growling when she went low. People pulled their trays away, and Iz stepped up on the table. Her wide eyes flashed. She paraded up and down, bending to stroke the hair and shoulders of all the cutest guys, and finished the number with her legs and arms wide, triumphant.

The cafeteria exploded into applause, and Iz glowed as she stepped off the table. Then she dropped Miss Adelaide's Brooklyn accent and turned to me: "I love that song. Don't you?"

"You have an awesome voice," I said. Because it was true. Because I liked Iz, even though I also hated her.

Because what she'd just done, though obnoxious, was also exciting. She wasn't just a brassy girl who talked big. She lived big, too. Sang big. It was thrilling that someone who looked so ordinary had so much light inside her.

But could I ever win a part she'd set her sights on?

WE HAD the afternoon free, and the sun was out. People sat on the grass outside the dorms, singing snatches of show tunes and lying with their heads on each other's stomachs. Everyone was lolling around, the girls showing off their legs, the boys taking off their shirts, topping each other with stories of the plays they'd done in high school, the speech competitions they'd won, the parts they aimed for someday—and bonding. All of us were dreaming the exact same dreams.

Nanette squeezed in on a cotton blanket between me and Demi and started feeding us Skittles with her tiny fingers. Iz came up and leaned on Nanette's legs, demanding to be fed as well. Then we all lay on our backs and kicked our legs to the sky like Rockettes while trying to remember the lyrics to "All About

Ruprecht" from *Dirty Rotten Scoundrels*. Demi demanded we airplane him, which we did, and then he tried to fly on our feet and catch Skittles in his mouth at the same time, which ended in disgustingness.

Theater folk are like this, I realized. Physical right away. Kissy, huggy. Not like my family at all. Theater people will act like your oldest friend when you've just met. And they do it even while they're competing with you.

That night, there was a dance in the black box theater: sweaty, dark, a blur. Demi got filled with testosterone as soon as he heard "My Humps," and chased Blake all night. He was surprisingly unslick in his adoration. He pulled Blake outside to look at the "incredible moon" and gyrated next to him with ridiculous abandon. As if he were marking his territory. All the gay boys were eyeing the two of them, as well as the girls who were thus far clueless as to their orientation.

I danced, and danced, and danced. After the agonies and excitements of the day, I just moved, letting the music go through me. I danced with Demi, Lyle, Iz, Nanette, Candie, and even Blake. I danced by myself when other people got tired.

I didn't dance with Theo, though. When I finally spotted him, he was holed up in one corner, talking intently to a girl named Bec. A Kristinish brunette with a turned-up nose.

Bleh.

Iz, Nanette, and I convened in the girls' bathroom.

"You should ask him to dance," Iz advised. "Guys like it when you ask them. I asked Wolf to dance at a club; did I tell you that's how we met?" She reached over and picked up my lip gloss, spreading it on her wide mouth without asking. "My skin is like, so broken out," she moaned, shoving her face up to the mirror. "It always breaks out when I have auditions."

Nanette pulled out gold glitter mascara and put some on her eyelashes, then handed it to me like of course I was going to use it. "We can't be dancing with the gay boys all night," she announced. "It's already been going on too long. If you ask Theo the piano player, Sadye, I'll ask that guy in the *Rent* T-shirt."

"What makes you sure *he's* not gay?" asked Iz.

"I've got no idea. But I'll find out, won't I?"

"I don't understand why Theo's all over *her* now," I said, going back to the subject of Bec. "One second he's walking me back to my dorm and practically barging his way in, the next second he's forgotten I exist."

"He's distracted, that's all," said Iz. "Straight guys here get an enormous amount of play. If you want him, Sadye, you've got to pounce."

"But I pounced earlier today. I shouldn't have to do all the pouncing. He should pounce me back."

"He did pounce you, he tried to come into the dorm room."

"But he's not pouncing now."

"Now he's pouncing Bec," Nanette put in. "So you have to repounce."

I took a deep breath. "I'll repounce if everyone pounces. Nanette, you do the *Rent* shirt guy. And Iz, you ask someone, too."

"Okay." Iz was surprisingly open for someone madly in love with Wolf. "I'll pounce that crew-cut guy with freckles, did you see him?"

"With the pierced ears?"

"Yeah."

We looked at ourselves in the mirror: Nanette, under five feet and dressed in white jeans and a white shirt, tons of makeup, and a swarm of strawberry hair curling in the humidity; Iz, curvy and broad-shouldered, wearing a red cotton sundress with a black bra peeking out; me, tall, a little androgynous, a lot glittery, in a green T-shirt that said "Natural Blonde" and my brown suede miniskirt. "We look fabulous," I said. "Let's pounce."

Theo was talking to a different girl from the one before. Well, that was encouraging. At least he hadn't proposed immediate marriage to Bec. Nanette gave me a slight shove in his direction, and I marched up and tapped his shoulder. "Come dance with me!"

"Hey, Sadye." Theo smiled. "Give me a minute."

"Okay."

He didn't introduce me to the girl.

He hadn't said no. Right? He'd basically said yes.

But what was I supposed to do? Stand there waiting?

For how long? And how far away from where he was talking to the other girl?

I waited for a minute, about five feet away, but Theo and the girl kept talking. And kept talking. So I started dancing, on the edge of the crowd, figuring Theo could find me when he was free. But before I'd been there twenty seconds, Demi came up and started doing some ridiculous shimmy thing at me, dragging me into the center of the crowd. I shimmied back, and then we did the bump, and when I looked back for Theo—he was gone.

Later, I saw him talking to yet another girl, and another, and another, and it was pretty clear that he was realizing how few attractive straight boys there were at Wildewood, and that he really had his pick of the litter—and didn't have to settle for gawky, geek-tastic me.

* * *

I STEPPED OUTSIDE to get some air. And there, leaning against a tree, was James/Kenickie.

We hadn't been introduced. Iz said he'd come by our dorm, like she'd asked him to, but I had been in Lyle's room so we never met.

"That's a joke, right?" he said, pointing to my T-shirt.

"Natural blonde?"

"You're not really."

I shook my head.

James smiled. "I thought maybe you dyed it or something."

"No. I'm as brunette as they come."

"I saw you dancing inside."

"I'm Sadye—roommates with Iz. She said you were Kenickie last year."

He nodded. "They called me Greased Lightnin' all summer."

"I don't think that's so bad."

"Not as bad as the guy they called Jesus."

"From *Godspell*?"

"No, that was the year before. *Jesus Christ Superstar.* He got into the part a little too much, know what I mean?"

"I can guess."

There was a lull in the conversation.

"Where are you from?" I finally asked.

"Somewhere I'd rather not go back to," he said.

"I know what you mean," I answered. "I've been here less than twenty-four hours and I feel like I'd die if I had to go back."

James chuckled. "There's not a lot of places like Wildewood."

"There's New York City," I said optimistically. "There's Broadway."

He looked at me, up and down. Like he was deciding whether I was attractive or not. And then he pounced. "Do you want to dance?"

"I always want to dance," I said.

And so we did, until the lights came up and one of the teachers barked that there were only five minutes until curfew.

THE NEXT morning was the Meat Market—otherwise known as Summer Institute Preliminary Monologues and Songs, otherwise known as auditions. They took place in the Kaufman Theater, and Nanette, Demi, and I got there early. We were each given a large paper number and a pin so we could attach it to our shirts. Farrell,

Demi's hall counselor and a voice major at Carnegie Mellon, stood by the door with a clipboard and made sure that our names and numbers matched up properly. "Keep your number through tomorrow!" he barked loudly. "You're going to need it! Don't throw it away or you'll have to have a makeshift one and everyone will know you lost it!"

When we had all assembled, Tamar taught the whole school an easy jazz combo, and then had us come up in groups of twenty to perform it four times, each time sending the front line to the back so new people could step up. Nanette was number fourteen, Demi was fifteen, and I was sixteen—so we were in the first group.

Nanette was good. I couldn't see her much out of the corner of my eye, but I could tell she had years of lessons behind her.

Demi was his usual ridiculous self, sticking his butt out and wiggling it like a lunatic when he messed up the steps.

I nailed it—if I do say so myself. We took our seats again, flush with the thrill of dancing to Kander and Ebb (the song was "All That Jazz") in front of more than a hundred people—and glad to have gone early because now we could watch the meat.

Blake from Boston was in the next group, and he looked ridiculous.

"Oh, I have to shut my eyes!" whispered Demi. "I'm losing all desire for that poor boy."

"Maybe you should keep them open." Lyle smirked, sitting a row behind us.

Demi covered his eyes with his hands but made a show of peeking through. "Oh, dear! Poor Blake. Maybe he can sing."

"He doesn't need to sing," said Lyle. "He just needs to stand there and the part of Conrad Birdie will fall at his feet." (Conrad Birdie is a slightly degenerate 1950s rock star—the title character in *Bye Bye Birdie*.)

"Why?" asked Demi.

"If he can't sing, won't they put him in the straight play?" I prodded, turning around to look at Lyle.

"They won't want to waste those looks on *Midsummer*, that's my prediction," said Lyle. "Nobody really attractive gets shunted off to the straight play at Wildewood."

"But why will he get Conrad?" I asked.

"Think it over," said Lyle. "He can't dance, so no *Cats*. The male leads in *Little Shop* are dorky or demented. In *Show Boat* it doesn't matter if they're cute or not, and that leaves *Birdie*. They need a guy a million teenage girls will wet their pants over. Singing is secondary."

"Birdie has big numbers," objected Nanette.

"Cute has power here," explained Lyle. "Wilde-wood is not always a meritocracy. Very often, it's a cute-ocracy. At least when it comes to the musicals."

"Oh."

"Don't worry." Lyle pointed at Demi. "*You'll* do just fine."

"Thanks a lot!" Nanette hit Lyle's knee playfully.

"No offense," returned Lyle. "You're extremely cute, too. Demi can be the king, and you can be the queen of the cute-ocracy. And maybe the meritocracy, too—if what I hear about your voice is true."

Nanette turned around in her seat, pleased.

Me, I knew better than to ask Lyle for a compliment. I'm a lot of things physically, and a lot of them are nice—but I am not cute.

"Now that he's not dancing, he looks better," whispered Demi, tilting his head toward Blake, who was back in his chair with his feet on the seat in front of him.

We watched dancers 41–60 go through the combination.

(click . . . buzz of people whispering, sound of piano in the background thumping out "All That Jazz" over and over)

Demi: *(sotto voce)* Ooh, you brought the minirecorder!

Sadye: *(whispering)* Micro.

Demi: Whatever. Okay, the date is June twenty-sixth, and we're watching the dance combinations that go before preliminary monologues and songs.

Sadye: In other words, we're at the Meat Market.

Demi: But I know what meat I want already. I want that Boston meat.

Sadye: Gross!

Demi: You're right. That did sound gross.

Sadye: Don't get distracted by meat. Tell posterity what is happening.

Demi: People are dancing onstage. Monsieur le petit Howard has decided not to sing "Manchester, England."

Sadye: You what?

Demi: I brought extra sheet music, in case I needed to change.

Sadye: I would never have thought of that. What are you changing to?

Nanette: *(leaning in to look at*

the microcassette recorder) Is
that machine on? What are you
doing?

Demi: We're recording our
experiences for posterity.

Sadye: In case we're famous some
day.

Demi: *Because* we'll be famous some
day.

Sadye: It's like a document.

Demi: I'm a seat away from Nanette
. . . Hey, what's your last name?

Nanette: *(no response, watching
the dancers)*

Sadye: Nanette, Demi wants to
know, what's your last name?

Nanette: Wypejewski, but I go by
Watson. It's easier to remember.

Demi: Maybe she should just be
Nanette, with no last name.

Sadye: That's a bit much, don't
you think?

Demi: Anyway, Nanette Watson is
here with us, and behind me is
Lyle, former first mate of the
Jolly Roger.

Sadye: *(watching the dancers, too)*
Even the best guys lose their

appeal when you see them trying to dance. It's skewing my Meat Market experience.

Nanette: You are so right. Is that your Theo guy?

Sadye: Number forty-three.

Nanette: So do you like him, or what?

Sadye: What do you think? Do you think he's cute?

Demi: You asked me that yesterday.

Sadye: So?

Demi: He dances like a straight boy.

Sadye: That's because he's straight.

Demi: He doesn't have to dance like it. There's no call for *that*.

Sadye: But do you approve, is what I'm saying.

Demi: Miss Sadye, you act like personality isn't important. You act like I'd judge a book by its cover!

Sadye: Yeah, yeah, yeah. What do you think of his cover, though?

Demi: His pants are too baggy. I

can't see his buns. Maybe
he's hiding something under
there.

Sadye: Demi!

Demi: You asked!

Sadye: He's not hiding anything,
sheesh.

Demi: How do you know? He is most
certainly keeping the shape of
his buns a secret.

Sadye: He can play anything you
want on the piano. Anything.

Demi: I'm reserving judgment
until he wears some tighter
pants.

Sadye: Shut up.

Demi: I can tell you like him.
That was a test just now, to see
if you got upset. If you got
upset that meant you really
liked him.

Sadye: Right.

Demi: You passed, by the way.

Sadye: I need a plan to make him
notice me. It's like he noticed
me, noticed me again, and then
un-noticed me.

Nanette: He un-noticed you?

Sadye: Exactly. Reverse noticing.
Anti-noticing.

Nanette: So now you need him to
re-notice you.

Sadye: Yeah.

Nanette: One thing I do when I'm
auditioning is wear this long
scarf, see? It helps give
directors a way to remember me
easily. The girl in the scarf,
if they can't remember my name.

Sadye: I'm not going to wear a
scarf. It's like eighty degrees
out.

Nanette: It was an *idea*. Not a
scarf. Something *like* a scarf.

Sadye: Whatever.

Nanette: Oh, there's Kenickie.
He's a hetero boy.

Demi: Who's Kenickie?

Sadye: Number sixty-one. His real
name is James. I danced with him
yesterday.

Demi: He dances like a Timberlake.
That's not theater dancing.

Nanette: He's the one that likes
mint chocolate chip.

Demi: What?

Sadye: You missed it. I'm mint chocolate chip ice cream. As opposed to Brenton-variety vanilla.

Demi: So he has a thing for you?

Nanette: Yes.

Sadye: No.

Demi: Which is it?

Sadye: Iz thinks I'm his type. And he asked me to dance.

Demi: Oooh! The Timberlakian.

Sadye: You're going to turn me off him if you keep saying that.

Demi: Timberlakian, Timberlakian!

Sadye: Shut up!

Demi: He's okay, but I thought you liked the one that hides his buns.

Nanette: Kenickie has nice buns, but he's not my type.

Demi: What do you think, Sadye? Do you like the Timberlakian buns?

Sadye: At least he danced with me.

Nanette: Go where the bread is buttered, that's what I say.

Sadye: No one said it was buttered, though.

Nanette: Iz thinks it is.

Demi: The Timberlakian is covered in butter, Sadye! And the bun-hiding guy--he's like dry toast, that's what he is.

Sadye: (*sighing*) Let's return to our posterity agenda.

Demi: Fine, if we must.

Nanette: If we must.

Sadye: For the record, let it show that I am doing my anti-Kristinish "Popular" and Juliet, same as before. Nanette, what are you doing?

Nanette: "Tomorrow" from *Annie*. And *The Bad Seed* for the monologue.

Sadye: And Demi, what are you doing, if you're not doing "Manchester"?

Demi: I think I have to shake it. So I don't get stuck with "Ol' Man River."

Sadye: Shake what?

Demi: My booty.

Sadye: You are obsessed with buns today.

Demi: Not just today, darling.

Sadye: So what are you singing?

Demi: Wait and see.

Sadye: What?

Demi: That's all I'm saying.

Sadye: If you're not going to tell your audition piece to the microcassette, I'm turning it off.

Demi: Ooh, look at Iz. She can dance. Oh, and poor, poor Candie.

(silence, with only the sound of "All That Jazz" still coming from the piano)

(shuffle, thump, click)

I NEVER GOT to hear whether Blake could sing. I never heard Theo or James, either. When the dance combinations were over, we broke for lunch and returned to see Reanne at the microphone.

"Here's the drill," she said, pushing a strand of gray-blond hair out of her face. "When your group of twenty is called, you'll wait in line by the edge of the stage. On your turn, you come up, give your sheet music to Robert here, and say your name and number loudly. Then start with your *monologue*. That gives

Robert a moment to prep. The monologue is to be two minutes long. When your time is up, you'll hear me say 'Thank you,' even if you haven't got to the end. Don't be offended, it's a matter of keeping us all on schedule. When he hears that 'Thank you,' Robert will play the intro to your song. Sixteen bars, and you're done. Collect your sheet music and exit off stage left, and back to your seat. If you don't have sheet music, sing a capella. That's no problem. And no, you can't go back to your dorm and get the music if you forgot it. Too chaotic. Okay, let's go."

Up we went, numbers one to twenty, and sat in the red-carpeted aisle, directly in front of a short flight of steps that led to the stage. My hands were sweaty and I looked over my music again, though there was really no point. I couldn't read the notes.

The first few people up were unremarkable—nice, on-key voices, solid acting. But nothing special. Poor number five forgot his lines and made jokes. Six, seven, eight, nine, ten—all of them could sing, though nine had picked a song with a note she couldn't reach. Eleven was unimpressive. Twelve cried during a monologue about a dead baby but then sang off-key ("Straight play!" whispered Nanette)—and then thirteen was Bec, the brunette with the turned-up nose who flirted with Theo. And she sang my song. "Popular."

She was Kristinish in the extreme. Petite, soprano, a bright, clear voice. She hit every joke and every note.

I shook and looked down at my hands, trying to be calm, telling myself it didn't matter. It didn't matter. It didn't matter.

"Just remember, you don't have to be like all the others," whispered Demi, squeezing my shoulder. "It's not important what you sing. Because none of these girls is Sadye Paulson. Only you are her. She. Whatever. The point is, only you."

I love Demi.

I took deep breaths, in and out.

Nanette (number fourteen) did her speech from *The Bad Seed*, in which she seemed like a truly evil little girl. Her acting style was broad—but she was well-rehearsed, loud as hell, and extremely confident onstage. Then she sang "Tomorrow"—and well, you already know she understudied that part in a national tour, so what else is there to say? Nanette got paid to sing onstage, and there was good reason for it.

I was so nervous I could barely breathe. I felt a cramp in my leg and stretched it out, grateful to be concentrating on something other than having to perform in front of all these people. When I looked up, Demi's *Top Dog/Underdog* monologue was nearly done—he was sweaty and full of passion.

Then he sang.

A song I'd heard him sing a thousand times—on the street, on the bus, whenever he was feeling down—but not one I'd ever dreamed he'd sing for an audition.

Liza.

Demi Howard was singing a Liza Minnelli song—"Cabaret." He'd had the pianist bring it down an octave, and he was belting it out like a total diva, singing how life is a cabaret, and you might as well live big. What good is sitting alone in your room? It'll all be over soon enough. You'll be dead eventually. We all will. So live wild and fast and hard while you can.

True, a few people tittered when they realized what he was singing—but they shut up when they saw how good he was.

So, so good.

It was supposed to be sixteen bars, but the pianist kept playing and Reanne didn't cut him off. Demi sang all the way to the end, selling the song like his life depended on it—and when he was through, half the audience applauded, though we weren't supposed to.

Demi jogged over to collect his music from Robert, and disappeared back into the throng.

* * *

I WAS UP.

Juliet. I'd gotten into Wildewood with it. But that was in a small rehearsal room, in front of only four people. Very different from standing alone onstage in a four-hundred-seat theater.

Remember, I had no training at all. No technique as an actress. As I began the monologue—"O Romeo, Romeo! wherefore art thou Romeo?"—I could hear how thin and dry my voice sounded. I kept talking and tried to speak louder, but my throat felt closed, and then I thought, I shouldn't be thinking about my throat and how loud I am, I should be thinking like Juliet.

I tried to remember how I wanted something—a good part, Theo for a boyfriend, a solo in a musical, a life away from Ohio—but instead of really wanting it, I was only thinking how I *should* want it now, and listening to how small my voice was, and wondering, suddenly, what to do with my hands.

I wasn't Juliet. I wasn't even Sadye speaking through Juliet.

I was just a person saying a collection of words as loud as I could in a memorized order. Words that had meant something emotional to millions of audience members over hundreds of years, but which meant nothing at all now. Because I made them mean nothing.

It was over before the two minute limit. I had timed it repeatedly at 1:45, so I knew I wouldn't get interrupted.

The piano tinkled the opening notes of "Popular" and I struck the pose I'd planned to start with. I growled out the first few lines of the song—but it was like I could hear Kristin's sunshine voice in my head, and beneath that, the soprano-voiced, piggy-nose Bec who'd gone before me—and I couldn't hear myself.

Couldn't hear how I should sing it, couldn't find the notes.

I'd choreographed a dance, figuring to play again to my strengths, and had practiced it over and over in the mirror at home. But as I did it now, it felt mechanical. My movements didn't come out of the music; I couldn't feel the rhythm and let it push me along, the way any halfway decent dancer can.

The whole song was flat and awkward and plain bad. I could tell it was even as I was doing it, and that made it worse.

When Reanne finally said "Thank you," I grabbed my music and ran off the stage, up the aisle, and out the door. We weren't supposed to leave, but I didn't care. I'd humiliated myself in front of all these people who would now know that I was an utter poser.

I mean, I'd consistently behaved like I was on a

level with Iz and Nanette. Doing walkovers in the sand. Acting condescending about Shakespeare and dance classes. Saying I wanted to play Miss Adelaide.

What had I been thinking? These were people who'd been on Broadway, or at the least starred in their school musicals. And let's get real: what had I done? Danced the blue-dress solo in the *West Side Story* medley at Miss Delilah's annual concert.

I rushed out of the dark, air-conditioned theater into the blazing sun. It was strangely quiet outside. The soundproof doors didn't let anything through. I sat on a stone bench a few yards from the front of the building.

Demi would come outside for me soon, I was sure—and though my face felt hot at the thought of my failure next to his success, I still wanted to feel his arm around me and hear him tell me that I'd been wonderful, that I was wrong about it going badly, that I was Sadye Paulson, and I was going to be famous, and I was a fabulous wondergirl, and Jacob Morales was an idiot if he couldn't see my talent.

But Demi didn't come.

And didn't come.

Maybe he'd been stopped by one of the teachers while coming out. Maybe something happened and he couldn't get to me.

Or maybe—he wasn't coming.

Thing was, in all the time I'd spent with Demi, especially since we got our Wildewood acceptances, I'd been thinking of myself as special. As charged with talent. As big.

Demi believed in me, and I'd begun to believe in myself.

Only now, after what I'd done—how could I?

(click, shuffle)

    Sadye: We're in the cafeteria, posterity, so forgive the noise levels.

    Demi: Me, Nanette, Lyle, Iz, and Sadye are consuming potato products and discussing the Meat Market.

    Nanette: Sadye is depressed, so we convinced her to listen to audition horror stories from our disreputable pasts.

    Sadye: Darlings, I'm fine, really. I can keep my chin up.

    Demi: You were good. It was just an off day.

    Sadye: How can it be both?

    Demi: I don't know.

Sadye: It can't be both.

Demi: Don't jump on me, darling. I'm trying to say the right thing.

Lyle: It happens to everyone. Auditioning is like a weird skill that's not even the same as acting.

Nanette: Exactly. There are great actors who audition badly.

Sadye: Then how do they ever get parts?

Lyle: They just do. They get better, or word of mouth gets around, or directors see something in them even though they messed up. Last year, there was a guy--oh, that guy Dean, you see him over there in the black shirt? His voice cracked so bad in his audition he ran off the stage and forgot his sheet music. The piano player had to chase after him. And he got Doody in *Grease* and, um, let me think, a decent part in *South Pacific*. So it can happen.

Nanette: When I auditioned for

Beauty, I was so nervous I wet my pants a little in the waiting room. Like the seat underneath me was wet.

Iz: Gross!

Nanette: I know. Don't go telling people.

Lyle: *Beauty* what?

Sadye: She was in *Beauty and the Beast*.

Nanette: On Broadway. Anyway, it wasn't exactly wet, but damp, you know? And I was scared to change seats, and too scared to tell my dad what happened. I didn't want to go to the bathroom in case they called my name while I was there, so--

Demi: Wait, how old were you?

Nanette: Eight. I know. Really too old to be wetting your pants.

Iz: That is so gross. So did you sing wearing wet clothes?

Nanette: I did.

Sadye: And then you got it?

Nanette: I got the understudy. Then later I stepped into it.

Lyle: So there you go. Wet pants

and a success story.

Iz: When I tried out for *Born
Yesterday* at my performing arts
school, I had too much drool in
my mouth. I was halfway through
the scene we were supposed to
do, and I realized there was a
string of drool that went like,
all the way from my mouth to
almost my knee. I am dead
serious.

Demi: What did you do?

Iz: I pretended to drop my script
and wiped it off. But I was so
sure I wasn't going to get the
part.

Sadye: But she did. She told me
she played--what's the character
called?

Iz: Billie Dawn.

Lyle: Another success story with
bodily fluids. See, Sadye? It'll
be fine. You didn't even lose
control of your functions.

Sadye: Thank goodness for small
miracles.

Lyle: My first year at Wildewood,
I was only like, fourteen, and

I went up on my lines in a monologue. I was trying out for *The Front Page* and I--I don't even remember what speech I was doing, but I had no idea what came next. Just stood there, stuttering, until the director asked me if I wanted to take it again from the top.

Demi: And did you?

Lyle: I would have--because you've got to get back on the horse--only I couldn't remember the beginning of it anymore, either. I was a complete blank. So they said "Thank you very much" and sent me out.

Sadye: Did you get the part?

Lyle: No way. I was barely in anything that whole first year.

Sadye: That's not encouraging!

Lyle: Yes, it is. Because look, here I am. I did five shows last year, and no one remembers what happened back then. Except me.

Demi: Do you feel better now, Sadye? Tell us you feel better.

Sadye: Okay, okay. I feel better.

```
        If you let me have the rest of
        your French fries.
     Demi: Good.
     Sadye: I'm as better as I can
        feel, anyway.
   (click)
```

T HAT NIGHT we saw an all-teacher performance of *The Importance of Being Earnest*, done in the black box theater. Theo was there, of course, and so was James. But I ignored them both after my humiliation at the auditions. It was easier to stay with Demi and Lyle, who liked me for my personality rather than for my (at this point highly questionable) talent or (apparently limited) sex appeal. All I wanted was not to think about how badly I'd done and how stupid I must have looked.

After the show we stood outside in the crickety night, leaning against the brick wall of the building and watching the Wilders mill around. None of us was ready to go back to the dorms since there was nearly an hour before curfew.

"There's an all-night convenience store two blocks off campus," Lyle mentioned. "They'll sell me beer, if you guys feel like making a run."

"Do you have an ID?" asked Demi.

"No. They're lax. If they didn't sell to kids from Wildewood, they'd have hardly any business. What do you say?"

I shook my head. I could tell the invitation was meant as a temptation for Demi, not me. Besides, I'm not much of a drinker.

Demi tilted his head at Lyle, looking out of narrowed eyes. "Isn't that the sort of escapade that can get you kicked out of here?"

"Actually," said Lyle, "this guy on my hall got booted a couple months ago for having a bottle of whiskey in his locker. But darling, wasn't it you who said life is a cabaret?"

"That doesn't mean I'm risking expulsion."

"No way is Farrell going to catch us, and if he does, he won't *do* anything," said Lyle. "He'll just take our beer and drink it himself."

Demi looked tempted, and Lyle went on:

"I've got the run down to eighteen minutes, door-to-door, if you go over the stone wall at the south end of campus. We timed it with a stopwatch last term."

I thought Demi was going to say yes, because he's never one to turn down adventure, but then Blake came up to us.

Blake, who had a chain of bright blue beads around

his neck, surfer-style; Blake, who had ignored Demi all day, flirting with girls and boys alike in the front row, where we could see everything he did; gorgeous, selfish Blake came up and flirtatiously banged his shoulder into Demi's. "Hey, where you been?" he asked.

Like we hadn't been down the table from him at dinner, and behind him in the theater.

Demi turned on his smile. "Bunburying."

(This was a joke from *The Importance of Being Earnest*, and I should explain it since there was a lot of Bunburying going on at Wildewood. In the play, whenever a guy named Algernon wants to escape social obligations, he claims he's got to go and visit his sick friend Bunbury, who doesn't exist. Then he goes and does something he finds more entertaining than whatever he was obligated to do, and he calls this whole evasive maneuver "Bunburying." During the intermission that night, Lyle told us that they'd studied the play in English and that some people interpret the whole Bunbury motif as homosexual. Like, to Bunbury is to go off and have homosexual adventures while lying to your family about it—it's a code. So it means slagging off some obligation, *or* it means guys fooling around with each other, or it means both. Great word.)

Blake laughed and said, "I heard you can get up on the roof of the dance building, want to go check it out?"

"You used to be able to, but you can't anymore," said Lyle. "They alarmed the door at the top of the stairway ever since they found bottles up there."

Blake ignored him. So did Demi. "I'm in!" he said, running off across the quad. "Bet I beat you there!"

Blake laughed and chased Demi over the grass.

They were gone.

Lyle and I stood there. "Sorry," I finally muttered.

As if I could speak for Demi. And meaning, Sorry, he doesn't want you; Sorry he's so shallow; Sorry, I know you're worth a thousand Blakes; Sorry, he's never been anywhere like this where he can be out of the closet all the time and I think it's gone to his head; Sorry, it's like this in the world, with the beautiful people running off with each other. And also, Sorry, I wanted him to stay, too.

"You know what?" Lyle said thoughtfully, looking off in the direction they'd gone, although we couldn't see them any more. "It ain't over till the fat boy sings."

T WENTY MINUTES after I got into bed, my room-mates came in and woke me up. Candie was in a tizz because Nanette had told her there was no way she could sing "Memory" for her audition the next day. "Tell me why, again?" sniffed Candie plaintively, as she changed into a nightgown.

"It's unprofessional," said Nanette. "You can't sing a song from the show you're auditioning for. No one does it. You're not supposed to."

"But I didn't know they were doing *Cats*. They didn't tell us what they were doing till we got here!"

"You try to find out," said Nanette. "That's what I did. Or you look on the Web and see what they did last year and the year before, because you know they won't repeat those."

"You knew your agent, who knew Morales," put in Iz, walking through the room naked on her way into the shower. "I've been here two other summers and even *I* didn't know what they were doing."

"Do you have any other sheet music?" I asked Candie.

She shook her head.

"Okay, let's be practical," said Nanette. "What else can you sing?"

"Nothing." Candie buried her face in her pillow.

"You're a soprano," pushed Nanette. "You must know 'Somewhere Over the Rainbow.' Sing that."

"I don't think I know it. Not really."

"Or 'The Sound of Music'?"

Candie shook her head.

"You don't know 'The Sound of Music,' are you joking?"

"No."

"There must be something. 'I Could Have Danced All Night'? A song from *Jekyll & Hyde*?"

"Not a capella," said Candie. "I can't sing those a capella."

"Aw, leave her alone," I moaned. "She can sing 'Memory' if she wants to."

"Only if she wants to seem like she doesn't know what she's doing."

"There's nothing else she can do."

Candie was silent.

"I was just trying to help," huffed Nanette, getting into bed and pulling up the covers.

THE NEXT DAY of monologues and songs was like the first. A string of faces, all nervous.

Iz was fiery and cute onstage—much more attractive than she was up close, and she sang "Sandra Dee" with that gritty belt, and so much polish to the jokes and gestures that you could tell she'd done it in a real show the summer before.

The night before, Blake and Demi had failed to get on the roof of the dance building, as Lyle had predicted, but they'd kissed in the staircase until curfew. Which was probably Blake's plan in the first place.

"Just kissing?" I whispered to Demi as we sat in the audience.

Demi slapped my hand. "I've only known the boy two days! I'm saving myself for marriage."

"Uh-huh. Yeah."

"We have a whole lovely summer stretching out in front of us," said Demi dreamily. "Me and Blake, Blake and me."

I hoped he was right.

And then, if I'm being honest, I hoped he wasn't.

CANDIE WAS number 115—quite near the end—and she sat between me and Iz after lunch, when Demi went to sit with Blake. Her pink skin was sweaty, and she'd done her white-blond hair in a pair of pigtails that made her look like a farm girl. She didn't say a word, and I thought about how hard it must be to be so close to last, watching all those talented people take the stage.

Sitting there, I felt a kinship with her. Candie

and me, we were the also-rans here. Neither of us was exactly pretty, and neither of us could compete with girls like Iz—much less with girls like Nanette. We were the ones who should probably pack up our dreams, take them home with us at the end of the summer, and stick them down in our family's basements.

I resolved to be nicer to her even though she didn't thrill me—even though her needy spirit grated on me and made me want to shake her—because I was sure she felt the same way I did.

Candie's group was called, and I sat through two back-to-back renditions of "Out Tonight" from *Rent*, followed by one guy who attempted to sing a song from *Avenue Q* in which he pretended his two hands were Muppets, and a lame fellow whose singing was so bad that I don't even know what he sang.

Candie went up and stood center stage. "I forgot my sheet music," she said. "Or, well. Actually, I changed my song."

"That's all right," came Morales's thin, high voice. "Begin with the monologue, please."

Candie's speech was from *The Diary of Anne Frank*— and thing was, all her lack of self-consciousness—her *Jekyll* obsession, her ex-boyfriend hang-up, her awkward style, the fact that being around her was like being around an open, gaping wound and you wanted to beg her, please, to bandage herself up—it was brilliant onstage. She was honest.

And then she sang. A capella, she launched into "The Star-Spangled Banner."

Now, if you've ever had to sing that song in a school assembly, you'll know that it is really, really difficult. It goes way low down, and very high. The "rockets red glare" part is a disaster for most people. But Candie—her voice swooped up to the top notes like a dove. She tipped her soft, round face up to the balcony and raised her arms as she got to the end, every note creamy and clear.

"Well," muttered Iz. "She'll give Nanette a run for her money, now won't she?"

THE CAST LISTS were posted the next morning at eight a.m. on a kiosk in the center of campus. After we looked at them, we were supposed to proceed to breakfast and our first day of regular classes and rehearsals.

Nanette was too cool to go at eight and said she was going to take advantage of the empty bathroom, but Candie, Iz, and I ran out early. When we got there, the five posted lists were obscured by a crowd of people—nearly all of Wildewood was already there to see. The girls had no makeup, the boys had bed head. Everyone was squealing and jumping in glee, talking and clutching each other's arms. "We're together!" "I knew you'd get a good part!" "I'm so excited!" "It's gonna be a great show."

I looked for my name first on the list for *Little Shop of Horrors* (which has such a small cast that there are no bad parts), then on *Bye Bye Birdie* next to it.

Not on either one.

Then *Cats*, which wasn't a show I wanted, but which was such a dance-centered project I actually had a decent chance of getting a good part.

Not there either.

Then *Show Boat*.

No.

I looked again at *Cats*, thinking maybe I'd missed myself, since I wasn't used to seeing Sadye in print.

But no.

People were all around me, pushing and exclaiming. My throat closed up as I moved my way to the end of the bulletin board so I could scan the list for *Midsummer*.

There it was. Sadye Paulson.

I was playing a character I didn't even remember, though I'd read the play in English class. Peter Quince.

I was playing a man.

Apparently, I wasn't even recognizably female.

I wanted to be happy for my friends, but tears had made my cheeks wet before I even realized I was crying.

I tried to remember what Morales said about humility; about subduing the ego for the good of the show.

I tried to think that doing Shakespeare would be wonderful training for my career. I told myself I still had a long summer of acting classes and voice lessons and rehearsals—and that at least I was out of Ohio.

It just seemed so unfair, not to have what I'd been dreaming about for months.

Not to have a chance.

I could see Demi on the other side of the crowd, jumping up and down. He was playing the title character in *Bye Bye Birdie*—but I didn't go up with my congratulations. I knew I should, but I choked on the words and turned back toward the dorm.

That was my first mistake with him.

NANETTE WAS in our room, drying her hair. "How'd it go?" she asked.

I swallowed hard. "You wanna know what you got?"

"Don't tell me!"

"All right . . ."

"No, *do* tell me," she begged. And for once her hard face looked open.

"Julie in *Show Boat*."

It was a big part. Nanette danced around the room.

And at that moment, I hated her. She had everything I wanted.

Everything.

"Candie got Audrey in *Little Shop*," I said quietly. And I hated myself as I said it, even though I knew Nanette would find out eventually, because she stopped dancing and the hardness came back into her face.

I could see I'd taken away her moment of happiness. It was the part she had wanted.

"Someone had to get it." She shrugged.

But she wasn't that good of an actress.

I gave her the rest of the rundown. Demi as the rock star in *Bye Bye Birdie*. Iz as the fiery Latin secretary who dreams of a split-level house and marriage. Blake was playing a boring part in *Show Boat*.

Then I told her about *Midsummer*. "Lyle's in it with me," I said as cheerily as I could. "He's playing Bottom, so it should be kinda fun."

But underneath I was in a downward spiral, thinking, Everyone who can dance at *all* is in *Cats*, except me.

Am I not the dancer I thought I was?

Is my singing so bad that they won't even let me leap around in a stripy unitard because I'll pull the whole chorus off-key?

Why do they think I should play a man? I don't look like a man.

Do I?

Do I?

I shouldn't be here. My name got mixed up with someone else's, and some poor girl with loads of talent is sitting home somewhere in Ohio, rejected, when she should be here instead of me.

"Earth to Sadye," barked Nanette. "What about the ten-day wonder, sweet pea? Are we in it?"

I was startled out of my misery. I didn't know.

How could I not know? How could I not have checked?

"We have to go find out," said Nanette. "Come on!"

So back we went, and heard that Reanne hadn't posted the ten-day wonder cast until eight thirty—explaining to the cluster of Wilders who stood around the bulletin board that Morales had left his final decisions until the morning, which is why it went up late.

Nanette was the long-suffering cabaret performer, Miss Adelaide. Candie had the other female lead: Sarah, an upright mission worker who falls in love with a handsome rake of a gambler, Sky Masterson—to be played by Demi.

Lyle was small-time thug Nicely-Nicely Johnson, and Blake played a police officer, Lieutenant Brannigan. Theo was Benny Southstreet, another gambler who opens the show singing a trio, "Fugue for Tinhorns." James was Rusty Charlie.

And there, down at the bottom under Dancing Hot Box Girls, was my name. Sadye Paulson.

I was in.

In the ten-day wonder. Directed by Jacob Morales, of the Broadway big time.

And for that moment, though it was short-lived, I didn't care if I didn't have a speaking part, didn't care if I wasn't a lead, didn't care. Because in was in was in was in.

WILDEWOOD SUMMER INSTITUTE SCHEDULE
Sadye Paulson
8 a.m. Breakfast
9–10:30 MWF: Advanced Dance (Sutton)
T/Th/Sat: Acting (Morales)
10:45–12 MWF: Pantomime (Ellerby)
T/Th/Sat: Singing (De Witt)
12–1 Lunch
1–5 Afternoon Rehearsal

5:15–6:30 MWF: Stage Combat (Smith)

T/Th/Sat: Restoration Comedy (Kurtz)

6:45 Dinner

8:30–10:30 p.m. Evening Recreation/Evening
  Rehearsal

11:30 p.m. Curfew

I HAD MORALES for Acting, nine a.m.—but I was late. I had been looking forward to the class since I'd first seen my schedule, and was even more excited now that I knew I was in his show—but the lines at breakfast were long, because everyone had stayed outside waiting for the *Guys and Dolls* list to go up. We only had twenty minutes to get food and eat, and I knew I wouldn't make it through my classes if I didn't eat at least a yogurt.

It was 9:05 when I got through the door. Morales was seated on a stool, lecturing a crowd of twenty students who sat on the floor of the classroom. He stopped when I entered.

"We've done the introductions already." His eyes were steely. "And you are?"

"Sadye Paulson."

"Sadye, please join the group."

I sat down, and Morales waited until I was settled before he continued talking. "I see we are going to have to begin at the very, very beginning, instead of at the advanced level a group like this *should* be operating on. Why?" He looked at me directly. "Because, Sadye, when an actor is even five minutes late for rehearsal, the way you were late for class today, that actor is being unprofessional. She is compromising the forward momentum of the production she's been cast in, not only because she's wasted the five minutes of every member of her cast, the director, the choreographer, the assistant director, the assistant choreographer, and the stage manager, which easily amounts to wasting more than an hour— more than an hour, people!—but also because she's creating an environment where people don't care about what they're doing."

Demi, sitting next to me, patted my arm.

"If the spear-carrier in the back row is less than fully committed," continued Morales, "a production suffers. The ensemble creating the theatrical work begins to erode—and that erosion, that lack of total commitment, can be detected by the audience. Do you understand me?"

We all nodded.

"And the same holds true for acting class. For dance, for voice, for singing, for everything you do here, and for everything you do when you return home. The starting place must be your commitment, because without that, we cannot work. I cannot help you. That commitment exists in your heart, or even deeper—in your cells—but it also has to be in your feet. Because they get you here on time. Every day. The commitment exists in your shoulder bag, because you carry your scripts and your dance shoes, and everything else you need to learn your craft and create your art. It should exist in your memories, because you learn your lines days before you're required to be off-book. In your body, as you eat well and get enough sleep so you can participate to your best ability. *That* is the starting place. *That* is what you need to learn, and I'm sorry to see you starting off the summer like beginners instead of professionals"—at this point, several people gave me dirty looks—"but I hope and trust you have the drive and motivation to learn." Morales looked at his watch. "Because now we've lost fifteen minutes of our class period on this remedial lecture I've had to give you, and we don't have time for the acting exercise I had planned. Instead, I want all of you to find a space on the floor and lie quietly, using this time to think over what I've said, and renew your commitment in your cells. At the cellular level, people."

We stood up in silence, shuffling to find spaces on

the cool rehearsal room floor, and lie down. I wanted to curl into a ball and cry from embarrassment, but everyone else was peacefully on their backs, so I swallowed hard and did the same.

Morales, once we were settled, walked out of the room.

I lay there, my face still hot.

Then I got cold. The air-conditioning had been running for a while. I lifted up my head and looked at the clock. We lay there twenty minutes. Thirty. Forty.

Morales wasn't there. The girl next to me was asleep, but other people were looking at their hands, or stretching a bit. I wanted my sweatshirt out of my bag, but I was too scared Morales would come back in and chastise the whole group because I was uncommitted enough to move out of position. So I lay still, staring at the clock and hoping that Singing (next period) would be better.

At ten fifteen, Morales reentered the room. "You may sit up," he announced.

We did.

"I'm pleased to see you all still here, where I asked you to be," Morales said, gazing down at us. "That's a hopeful sign. A sign of trust and the beginning of our ensemble knitting together to make theater as a collective. See you again on Wednesday."

And with that, he walked out again.

(shuffle, bang, click)

Sadye: *(in a whisper)* It's June twenty-eighth, 11:35 p.m. After curfew on the first day of classes.

Demi: *(too loudly)* She's in the boys' dorm!

Sadye: Quiet!

Demi: *(more quietly)* We're in the laundry room, with the light off, so we won't get caught by Farrell. Sadye climbed in like a ninja.

Sadye: Your room is on the ground floor.

Demi: Okay, I'm just giving you some credit. She ninja'd into my room and scared the pants off Steve and John.

Sadye: Mark slept through the whole intrusion. He was literally snoring while I climbed in the window, and he never even moved. I was like right next to his head!

Demi: Then we scurried down the hall and hid in here.

Sadye: And why? For you, O

posterity. We vowed at lunch to record the events of today, so important for documentary purposes, but then Demi forgot.

Demi: I didn't forget. Rehearsal went over.

Sadye: We're both in the ten-day wonder, but I had to go to the dance studio to learn "Bushel and a Peck," while Demi did-- what did you do?

Demi: We read though the whole script and then the music director started work on "Luck Be a Lady." Hey, did you have Advanced Dance? Sadye is an advanced dancer and is in the advanced-type dancing class.

Sadye: No, it's tomorrow. I had Singing.

Demi: I had regular dance second period.

Sadye: How was it?

Demi: My buns are hurting. I'm not used to all those pliés and stuff.

Sadye: Ha-ha!

Demi: *(loudly)* I'm serious! I have extremely sore buns.

Sadye: Shh! Keep it down!

Demi: *(whispering)* Okay, it's
down. Now, for posterity, what
was your elective, and what is
your evaluation of it?

Sadye: Restoration Comedy. We
tried on corsets.

Demi: On the first day?

Sadye: Yeah. We put on corsets and
then walked around, trying to
get the flavor of movement in
the Restoration era.

Demi: What did the guys do?

Sadye: There was just one. He
watched our heaving bosoms with
considerable interest. What was
yours?

Demi: I don't have bosoms.

Sadye: Your elective.

Demi: Audition Prep, and we had to
list our three most castable
qualities.

Sadye: What?

Demi: Our most castable qualities.
So we can capitalize on them to
find the best songs. Like: Comic
Relief, Tough Guy, Ingenue, High
Soprano, stuff like that.

Sadye: And yours are?

Demi: I said Joie de Vivre.

Sadye: Good one.

Demi: And Falsetto. But the instructor said that was too narrow. I could have an audition song with falsetto, she said, but I wouldn't always want to use it.

Sadye: And what was your last one?

Demi: Not telling.

Sadye: *(pinching him)* What do you mean, not telling?

Demi: Ow, ow!

Sadye: Tell!

Demi: Okay, it just sounds dumb. I said Leading Man Quality.

Sadye: And what did she say?

Demi: *(pausing)* She actually said that was fine, but I should replace Falsetto with Black.

Sadye: Why?

Demi: I'm black. Don't tell me you hadn't noticed!

Sadye: What?

Demi: I'm b-l-a-c-k, black.

Sadye: That's a mean thing to say.

Demi: Well--

Sadye: Why would you say that to me just now?

Demi: --because you act like you never noticed.

Sadye: What? You mean all the time?

Demi: Basically.

Sadye: How else am I supposed to act?

Demi: *(silence)*

Sadye: What, you want me to mention it every now and then, like, oh, you're looking especially black today, Demi? Or what?

Demi: No.

Sadye: Then what?

Demi: Don't get all huffy.

Sadye: I don't know what you're saying to me.

Demi: Other people mention it. Like they're not afraid to have it come up.

Sadye: Like who?

Demi: Lyle. We had a whole conversation after M-TAP today. Or like Candie, who--

Sadye: Candie's ridiculous.

Demi: Maybe so, but she came out front and asked if I was gay, didn't she? And later she told me she'd never had a black friend. She's being open about where she's coming from, even if she's clueless.

Sadye: But I don't notice that you're black. I don't.

Demi: That's what I'm saying. It's a huge part of me, and you don't notice.

Sadye: But isn't it good that I don't notice?

Demi: It's a fact. Hello, Sadye.

Sadye: Okay, it's a fact. And it's a fact I'm white. It's a fact I'm tall.

Demi: Not the same.

Sadye: Why not?

Demi: You can't say it's the same. You have to know that.

Sadye: *(silence)*

Demi: Anyway.

Sadye: Anyway.

Demi: The teacher said that people will consider casting me for certain parts because I'm black, and I should have a song in my repertoire that puts me in consideration for those roles.

Sadye: Oh.

Demi: Like a number from *Ragtime*. Or *Porgy and Bess*.

Sadye: Oh.

Demi: Whatever. I wonder what Brian Stokes Mitchell auditions with.

Sadye: Let's talk about something else.

Demi: Acting class. We had it together, with Mr. Morales.

Sadye: Oh, that was awful.

Demi: What?

Sadye: Hello? I was like five minutes late and he laid into me in front of everybody.

Demi: I thought you liked the man. You liked him after orientation.

Sadye: I do like him. That's why it was so bad. He's like this amazingly talented director, so it makes it all worse.

Demi: But why was it awful?

Sadye: Couldn't he cut me some slack? I was recovering from the

Midsummer horror. And we were
all late for breakfast because
of him putting up his cast list
late. I would never have been
late if I wasn't waiting for him
in the first place.

Demi: For what it's worth, I think
you were shafted with that Peter
Quince part.

Sadye: Thank you. But what I'm
saying is, given that it's the
first day and the cast lists
went up and it was like the
biggest drama for everyone,
not just me, so we were all
vulnerable, was it really
necessary for Morales to single
someone out for humiliation and
give us all a lecture?

Demi: Well--

Sadye: What?

Demi: Don't think I'm being mean,
but--

Sadye: What?

Demi: Yes, it was.

Sadye: What do you mean?

Demi: That was his whole point,
wasn't it? That it doesn't

matter if the cast lists went up, or your landlord kicked you out, or your wife left you, or whatever; a professional actor shows up on time and doesn't let personal life get in the way.

Sadye: Maybe. All right. But he didn't have to cancel the acting exercise and force us to lie on the floor for fifty-five minutes.

Demi: That was amazing. I had to pee so bad, but it was still amazing.

Sadye: What?

Demi: Nobody, not one single teacher, ever made me just think for an hour before. Really think about what's important.

Sadye: I wanted to learn something. Not lie on my back, wondering, When is he coming back, and did I ruin the class for everybody?

Demi: You didn't ruin it. He would have done that anyway, because that was like his whole point.

Sadye: What?

Demi: Trust. You have to trust your director, trust your acting teacher. He's the one who can see the whole picture, who can see how what you're doing fits into the scene, or the show. We had to trust that he hadn't forgotten us. Keep doing what he told us to do, even if it seemed bizarre. He was showing us we had to trust his vision.

Sadye: But he was probably outside smoking cigarettes and reading magazines while he was supposed to be teaching us acting.

Demi: He *was* teaching us acting. That's what I'm saying.

Sadye: It was a waste of time.

Demi: That's because you didn't do it properly.

Sadye: Why are you being so mean to me today?

Demi: What, are you still huffy?

Sadye: You're being mean.

Demi: Me? I'm the one who should be mad.

(There is a loud knock on the
    laundry room door. More like a
    bang.)

Sadye: Ah!

Demi: Hide, hide!

Sadye: Where?

Demi: There's nowhere--

Farrell, the hall counselor:
(opening the door and flipping on
the overhead light) What have we
here?

Demi: It's not what it looks like.
(shuffle, bang, click)

F ARRELL barged in on us.

We made excuses.

He kept shaking his head. But fortunately, he was the assistant director on *Bye Bye Birdie*—so inclined to be lenient with Demi. He let us off with a warning and marched me back to my dorm room, promising that he wouldn't report me for this first infraction.

* * *

DEMI AND I made up the next morning at breakfast. "Sorry I was such a pissant," he said, hugging me from behind as I stood in line for pancakes.

"Sorry I was such a wench."

"We okay?"

"Of course."

"Good. Does that mean I can eat some of your pancakes?"

"Stand in line yourself!"

"Oh, don't you want to give me a goodwill pancake? After we had our First Official Quarrel?"

"Okay, okay. But go get me some orange juice, all right?"

"Your wish is my command."

And we were back to our usual selves—but still. It *was* our First Official Quarrel—and it wouldn't be the last, it turned out.

THE NEXT few days were a blur of scripts, rehearsals, new classes, sweat, music, and dance. So much dance my feet bled and our bathroom was draped in dripping leotards we had rinsed out by hand. So much energy expended we gobbled two or even three peanut-butter sandwiches at lunch.

In *Midsummer* rehearsals we weren't spending much time with the script. We were bonding with trees.

Reanne's concept for the show, she told us, was that *Midsummer* was the ultimate ensemble piece.

Our set would be a large, raked circle covered with brilliant green canvas, and together we would create the magical forest of Shakespeare's imagination. In the story, two pairs of teenage lovers lose themselves in the wild woods, where mischievous fairies enchant them. A group of "rude mechanicals" (laborers) are also in the forest, led by a dorky fellow called Peter Quince (me). One of the mechanicals, Bottom (Lyle), gets turned into a donkey and is seduced by the fairy queen. A night of madness ensues. Love, fury, mistaken identities, magical spells.

Reanne explained that she envisioned us immersing ourselves in the fairy spirit of Shakespeare's comedy, and that instead of having trees or rocks or bowers or whatever, we'd be making these set elements with our bodies, wrapping ourselves in the canvas and becoming the forest before the eyes of the audience. "The concept of the actors forming the stage environment with their bodies is always part of the way I work," she explained. "It's organic. It's inherently theatrical. And it communicates with the audience on a deep level."

The first couple days, we held rehearsal in the Shakespeare garden (full of all the herbs and plants ever mentioned in any of Shakespeare's plays), in the woods at the back of campus, or by the lakeshore—communing with the spirit of nature. We held hands in a circle and closed our eyes, creating an ensemble as we passed a hand-squeeze from one person to another. We stood in the woods and smelled the earthy fragrances and listened to the soft sounds of the leaves in the wind. Then we ourselves "became" trees, reaching our arms skyward, trying to inhabit the wooden yet flexible quality of the forest. We sat on the edge of the water, each of us searching within ourselves for a gesture we felt would capture the beauty of the scenery around us—a gesture we could then bring to the rehearsal room to convey the presence of capricious, wonderfully alive Mother Nature that was such a big part of Shakespeare's vision.

I liked the exercises. Reanne was warm and generous and full of enthusiasm. I liked focusing my thoughts, listening to her husky voice guiding us. One day we played tag in the woods, pretending to be fairies.

Stage Combat was my favorite elective. We learned

how to fake-punch someone, listened to lectures about different kinds of fake-blood delivery systems, and fought with swords. It was a popular class with the straight boy contingent, including Theo (who was playing Lysander, one of the lovers) and a few of the rude mechanicals from *Midsummer*.

I was the only girl, and the teacher didn't cut me any slack because of it. "Harder, Sadye!" he'd yell from the sidelines as I thrust my sword into someone's side. "Fight like your life depends on it!" We practiced falling, shot off guns loaded with caps, and fake-slapped each other, over and over.

On the second day of class (day four of rehearsals) I got to slap Theo, whom I'd been ignoring as hard as I could ever since he hadn't danced with me. The teacher assigned us to be partners.

Whack! So you un-noticed me.

Whack! So you don't think I'm pretty enough to dance with.

Whack! So you forgot I even asked you.

Whack! So you want someone Kristinish like Bec.

It felt good, I have to say. Even though I was hitting my own hand, I got to look in his handsome face, think about how bad he'd made me feel, haul my arm back to hit him, then watch him contort in simulated pain.

Whack! So you think it was all right for Morales to humiliate me.

Whack! So you're mad I don't care that you're black.

Whack! So you're running off with Blake.

Whack! So you're more talented than I am.

By the time my turn ended my head was muddled—I almost didn't know if it was Theo or Demi in front of me, and why was I thinking about Demi at all? I wasn't even mad at him anymore, was I? The teacher told us to switch roles, but I barely listened. Just stood there feeling this mix of fury and confusion.

It was Theo's turn to slap me. We went through the scenario three or four times without trouble, but then his hand slipped and he walloped me across the cheek, hard and loud.

I stumbled back, my face stinging and my breath ragged.

"I hit you for real!" Theo cried, putting his hand over his mouth in shock. "Are you okay? Are you okay?"

I stumbled to a chair and sat down.

"It's turning red. Are you okay?"

I couldn't speak.

"I'm so sorry. Can I get you an ice pack or something?"

"No, no," I finally answered. "Just let me sit for a second. I'm not a delicate flower or anything."

Theo looked at me. Hard. "I know you're not a delicate flower," he said. "That's what I like about you."

"You know, I think I *will* take an ice pack," I told him.

Theo scurried off to get me one and tell the teacher, and I sat with my head between my knees.

I felt like I was melting.

After that, Theo and I went back to talking. The two of us became partners whenever we sparred in Stage Combat, and joked around together in *Midsummer* rehearsals. He liked my company—that was pretty certain. But I don't think he had re-noticed me as a girl—because he didn't pounce. And I didn't either. Because, why wasn't *he* pouncing? There were so many girls at Wildewood, lolling about in tights and leotards, asking him to play piano on lunch break while they practiced their songs, calling to him across the quad. Was Theo the guy who really preferred vanilla and only flirted with mint chocolate chip when there was no vanilla in sight?

SOMETHING BECAME clear to me during *Midsummer* rehearsals in the days that followed: the end result of Reanne's ensemble process was that some of us were going to play trees.

It was also easy to see that the people playing Puck, Bottom, Titania, and the lovers were not going to have time. So the people with little parts were going to be treeing it up.

Meaning me.

Once we started working with the script, Reanne was so committed to her ensemble fairy spirit vision—the idea that we were all collectively creating the play at every moment, no matter who was speaking lines and who was being a tree—that she had us stand there with our arms held out while the actors playing the lovers rehearsed their speeches.

I don't know if you've ever stood still with your arms out for half an hour, but it is fantastically uncomfortable.

To give her credit, Reanne was appreciative. She gave notes to the trees, and talked to us about the kinds of tree shapes we needed to make in order to create the ambiance for a particular scene. Sometimes I was a menacing tree, sometimes protective, sometimes jolly or wild.

But let's face it. For a serious portion of my rehearsal time, I was a tree.

One day, while the lovers and royalty were working

on the start of the play (which takes place in a palace, not the enchanted forest), the mechanicals had been assigned to stroll once again through the campus woods and improvise in character, "forging bonds and developing the nuances of the characters' interpersonal relationships," said Reanne.

So we walked. Me, Lyle, and four character-actor guys: one pale and femmy (Flute), one hatchet-faced (Starveling), one horse-faced (Snout), and one seriously short (Snug).

"You wanna know something?" asked Lyle as we stepped into the cool of the woods.

"You're gonna tell us anyway," I said.

"I wouldn't care if I never saw another tree in my life."

"Ha!"

"I am treed-out already, my friend. And it's only six days in."

"Seriously," said the femmy fifteen-year-old playing Flute, the bellows-mender. "And you don't even have to *be* a tree, do you, Bottom? I have to be a tree for like hours while Oberon and Titania quarrel."

"Me too," complained Starveling.

"Are they talking in character right now?" whispered Snout. "Because Reanne said to."

"Not sure," said Snug. "Are you?"

"Not sure," answered Snout, and cracked up.

"I'm not a tree," admitted Lyle, "but you know what I'm gonna be now, in the scenes before the mechanicals go on? Reanne just told me."

"What?"

"A rock. I'm gonna ball myself up and be a rock. Hermia is gonna sit on me."

"Poor Lyle." I patted his arm.

"Not as poor as you, darling. I saw you treeing it up behind me yesterday. You looked like you were gonna faint."

"*I* almost did faint," moaned Starveling.

"Reanne does this every year," said Lyle. "There's no stopping her. Last year she directed *Oedipus Rex* and had the members of the chorus be the furniture. It was laughable. People were totally being tables, and everyone was dressed in white bed sheets."

"Oh, no."

"Oh, YES."

"Lyle is definitely not in character," muttered Snout.

"I can't tell anymore," said Snug.

"Or maybe he is?" said Snout.

"But Reanne's way too nice for anyone to say anything," Lyle went on. "And she does all the organization stuff for Morales, keeps it off his back so he can be the star director."

"Aha."

"Her approach is founded on some interesting theories about drama, actually," said Lyle. "They made us take theater history last year, and Andre Gregory, I think it was, did this famous *Alice in Wonderland* with the Manhattan Project in like 1970 that used people's bodies to create the wonderland. It was really cool. We saw pictures."

"You know what we should do?" I said. "I mean, complaining is one of my favorite things, I'm not knocking it. But shouldn't we stop complaining and try to make it better? It's early days for this show. It doesn't have to be *Bedsheet Oedipus*."

"But how?" piped up Flute.

"Talk to her. We should make suggestions."

"That's not an actor's job," said Lyle.

"But isn't she talking about the ensemble all the time? Don't you think she knows *Bedsheet Oedipus* was bad?"

Lyle shook his head. "Maybe she does and maybe she doesn't. But it's not our position to talk to her about it. The actor's job is to realize the director's vision. If her vision is bedsheets, her vision is bedsheets. It's not a situation where challenging authority does any good."

"But if it's an ensemble, we should have a voice. Each of us should have a say."

Lyle pushed his glasses back up his nose. "I don't think so, Sadye. The only thing we can do is talk about it behind her back."

CONTRARY TO being in *Midsummer*, being in the ten-day wonder—even in a small part like mine—was like being a member of royalty. I got pulled out of Singing for a costume fitting on only the second day, and felt a glow of specialness as I ducked out the door and headed for wardrobe. Once there, I stood along with the other Hot Box Girls being pinned into evening gowns with Velcro closures for "Take Back Your Mink," and tried on yellow-feathered dresses for "Bushel and a Peck." The costume mistress and her assistants fitted us for gold high heels, checked our stocking sizes, brought out piles of fake furs for us to slink around in—brown for us, and white for Nanette.

We were all due at rehearsal by 7:30 p.m.—an hour before anyone not in the ten-day wonder had to be at evening recreation, so we rushed through dinner, ran back to change clothes, bandaged our feet, and grabbed our scripts—and hurried out of the dorms on the way to the studios as everyone else trickled back from the cafeteria.

Then we worked. Sweated. Usually the Hot Box

Girls danced nonstop for two hours. For "Bushel and a Peck" we all carried rakes. We tapped them on the floor in rhythm, swung them around, jumped over them, used them like canes, leaned on them as we jumped. For "Take Back Your Mink," we did a synchronized semi-striptease, followed by a complicated tap routine. It wasn't easy for me—though I'd had years of tap lessons—and Nanette, who wasn't much of a tapper to start with, wolfed down her food every night and ran off to the dance studio to get in an extra half hour on the routine.

But here's the thing about Nanette Watson: by the fifth day of rehearsal, when Morales was coming to see the dance routines, she had it nailed and was doing it better than I was.

The director, who had been spending his afternoons and evenings rehearsing the principals and gangsters, waddled into the dance studio, waved hello without saying a word, and sat down on a bench to watch the dances.

You could tell Tamar was nervous. Even though she was his girlfriend. She put us through both numbers, calling out during "Mink" to explain what we were doing with our imaginary clothes. The music director, sitting behind the piano playing accompaniment, didn't say a word.

When we finished, Morales was silent for a moment. Then he said: "If you think you'll get a rise in anyone's pants doing it that way, you're mistaken. Do you *want* the audience to fall asleep, here? Do you? *Do you?*"

We shook our heads, no.

"Then take 'Mink' again from the top and give it some old-fashioned sex appeal," he said. "And what I mean by that is when Tamar has told you to stick your bottoms out, *stick them out*. When she's choreographed a jiggle, don't give me this tiny, afraid little shimmy— 'Ooh, I'm only sixteen, I don't know if I should be doing this'—don't give me that, because you're *dancers*, no one cares about your inhibitions, it's your job to make the thing sparkle. Dance it big!" he yelled. "Or there's no reason for you to be here."

We did the number again. Doing everything he said. And it was much better. We could all tell.

But did he have to be so mean? And kind of gross?

Morales wasn't done. "Another thing. The altos sound off. Girls, tell me. Who's off?"

Iz and the other girl singing alto both shook their heads.

Was it me?

Was it?

I didn't think it was me.

"Altos, sing your part," said the music director

in an even voice. "Sopranos, stay quiet."

We sang. It sounded odd without the sopranos singing the melody. I concentrated on the exact notes I was supposed to hit.

"It's that one!" Morales pointed at me. "Tall Hot Box. Get her on her notes," he said to the music director, "or have her lip-synch if she's never gonna get it. We can get someone in to do vocal filler from backstage if we have to. We've only got five days left."

The music director nodded.

"Oh, and Nanette?" Morales added. "You look great, sweetheart. You sound perfect. But I want you to see if you can give the whole thing another level by showing us that Miss Adelaide's bored and miserable with her job in the nightclub. She's sick of hoofing around in front of a lot of slimy guys at the age of forty, okay? She wants to get married and quit the business. Can you be bored out of your mind and make it funny?"

Nanette nodded.

"Okay," Morales said. "I gotta go look at 'Luck Be a Lady' in the next room." He nodded at Tamar. "When I get back, I wanna see 'Bushel' again. 'Mink' is okay, leave it till the clothes get here. Then we're gonna dismiss the girls, and Nanette will show me how 'Lament' is coming along."

"Check."

With Morales gone, the music director played the alto part on the piano for me three times, until it looked like I had it. But I never felt sure. Singing notes that weren't the melody wasn't easy for me—though everyone else seemed to do it just fine.

(click, shuffle)

Sadye: It's July second, after curfew. Iz and I are in bed. Nanette and Candie just came in.

Iz: Hot Box Girls get out earlier than principals.

Sadye: Nanette is naked.

Nanette: I'm getting in the shower! I smell, people!

Sadye: Candie is lying on the floor.

Candie: Don't mind me. I'll just die of exhaustion right here.

Sadye: How was it?

Candie: Good. But hard. It's like, he doesn't just want me to sing the notes, he wants me to sing the feelings at the same time. Only, the things she's feeling she doesn't know she's feeling, which makes it impossible to do right. It's like this character never says what she's truly thinking--except when she gets drunk.

Iz: You sound good. Did you see us listening in the door? Before they kicked us out.

Candie: I had to kiss Demi, also. Because we did the Havana scene. And like, I didn't have any mints. I haven't taken a shower since dance class this morning, and I ate the pepperoni pizza at dinner. I was scared he'd like, barf on me.

Iz: There should be a rule that they have to tell you when you're gonna be kissing. It sucks so bad if you're not prepared.

Candie: I haven't kissed anyone since my boyfriend from *Jekyll*, either. My ex-boyfriend. Anyway. And only one other guy before that. So it was bizarre.

Iz: Is he a good kisser?

Candie: *(giggles)*

Iz: What? Does that mean he's good?

Nanette: *(coming out of the shower wrapped in a towel)* Or did he barf?

Sadye: Nanette, he did not *barf*. That was an expression. Be nice.

Nanette: Okay, then what did he do? She's not telling us anything!

Iz: Weren't you there?

Nanette: No, I was doing "Sue Me" down the hall.

Candie: *(giggling again as she strips off her clothes and heads into the shower)* He stuck his tongue down my throat, actually.

Nanette: He did *not*, he did *not*!

Candie: He did!

Nanette: In the middle of the rehearsal room? With Morales and everyone looking on?

Candie: *(yelling from shower stall)* Yeah! Like he didn't know you were supposed to, you know, stage kiss!

Sadye: He did the jumbo pounce.

(laughter, all round)

Iz: *(to Sadye)* Do you think he's ever kissed a girl before?

Sadye: I don't know.

Iz: Did he ever kiss you?

Sadye: Ugh! No. We're like brother and sister.

Candie: He sings great, though. He truly does. I sound like a sheep next to him.

Sadye: You don't sound like a sheep. You sound like cherries jubilee.

Nanette: *(getting into bed)* Speaking of pouncing. I have had zero pouncing opportunities since this thing went into rehearsal. And my *Rent* shirt boy turned out to have a girlfriend.

Candie: *(drying herself)* We don't even have Sunday off. Everyone gets Sunday off except for ten-day wonder. We don't even get Fourth of July. So how can we pounce?

Sadye: I think we gotta pounce at lunch.

Candie: Why lunch?

Sadye: You've got some energy, you've got a little free time,

you're not in rehearsal. It's
impossible to pounce in rehearsal.

Nanette: I'm with you, there. But
I can't pounce when I'm covered
in French-fry grease and I smell
like sweat. I'd repulse the guy.
I need to take a shower before
the pounce.

Candie: *(getting into bed)* When do
we get to shower when we're not
like, immediately going to
sleep?

Sadye: That's my point. The guys
here have gotta accept that the
sweaty, French-fry pounce is all
they're going to get.

Nanette: Have you been pouncing,
Sadye? Is that what you're
telling us?

Iz: And wait, did you pounce
Kenickie James or Theo?

Nanette: One is covered in butter!
Don't forget!

Iz: Ooh! Did you do the lunchtime
jumbo pounce?

Sadye: Just because I'm friends
with Demi does NOT mean I do the
jumbo pounce.

Iz: Okay, okay.

Sadye: I'm talking out my back end, all right? I haven't pounced. But I still think it's a good idea.

Nanette: So you should do it. Show us how it's done.

Iz: But which one will she pounce?

Nanette: Covered in butter, that's all I'm saying.

Sadye: I'm turning this off now.

Iz: Ooh, I forgot you were recording.

(click)

ON NIGHTS when the Hot Box Girls got out early, we stood at the door of the main *Guys and Dolls* studio for a few minutes after, watching the principals rehearse their scenes. It was amazing to see Morales in action. For example, one evening we watched Demi and Candie sing "I'll Know"—a love duet.

Early in the scene, when Candie says "Chemistry?" and Demi says, "Yeah, chemistry," Morales told Demi to look at Candie for one long beat before speaking— and suddenly Demi seemed like he really was in love, rather than just talking about it. The director also asked Demi to slow the phrasing down a tad—and the song sounded more sincere. He had Candie look up at the sky and keep her feet together while she sang, and she became a devout mission worker, rather than a shy high school student.

The man knew what he was doing. Everything he said to the actors made the show stronger. He wasn't gentle and he wasn't kind; he was eminently practical. He had a clear vision and he was a master at getting the actors to execute it. "Bushel and a Peck," which we'd run a few more times until we got the Morales seal of approval, was a hundred times better with Nanette hinting at her boredom and exhaustion than it had been when she was unreservedly perky.

Now, I liked Reanne, I did. But she was no Morales. She was, in fact, losing control of her cast.

I was doing my best with Peter Quince. I had a few funny lines, at least, and Reanne was nice about my natural delivery of Shakespeare's language. Quince is trying to get his group of foolish layabout friends to rehearse a play—and he's a bit bossy, a bit shrill, full of frustration. But the first day we stood up to block it, the bad energy from having been trees all week made most of the mechanicals downright punchy. Flute and Starveling kept forgetting their movements, and Lyle and Snug were making jokes throughout the rehearsal. Snout was bouncing up and down and mouthing other people's lines, trying to get Flute to laugh. And succeeding.

Reanne asked them to "channel that chaotic energy into the chaos of the scene," but seemed unable to quiet them down enough so that we could get anything done. We started over with my initial speech, but Lyle was muttering behind me: "Maybe parents will object to my character's name. Should we change it to Eugene? To avoid offense. Or maybe Engelbert? Because we don't want our parents to think it's racy and pull us out of the institute."

I was standing downstage, script in hand, *knowing* I wasn't doing a good job, and I thought, This show is going to be another *Bedsheet Oedipus*. Nobody wants to be in it. People aren't concentrating. Teenagers wrapped in canvas with their arms sticking out do *not* create a fairy atmosphere, even if the teenagers are truly thinking about Mother Nature and struggling to convey her essence through posture. In fact, the teenagers are so sick of being trees they no longer give two cents about the whole production.

The concept doesn't work, I thought, because *Midsummer* is not really an ensemble play. We're not *all* supposed to be one with the fairy forest—lovers, sprites, mechanicals. We're supposed to be contrasting elements and counterpoint story lines. It's confusing this way, with everyone trying to channel the spirit of magic and not being sure what their speeches even mean. And here I am, trying to be a good sport and think like a tree and act like a man, trying to figure out my scene and what my character is thinking—and Lyle and Snug won't even shut up long enough for us to learn the stupid blocking.

How could Reanne work side by side with Morales every summer and not absorb a single ounce of his directorial skill? Wasn't there something I could say or do to make this show turn out better?

But then I remembered what Morales himself had said the night of orientation, and what Lyle and Demi had both said, in their own ways: actors have to be in bad shows all the time. They have to soldier on and do the best job they can do, because that's what a good actor does. He doesn't question the director or undermine the process, no matter what he thinks. He subdues the ego.

He commits.

* * *

James, Theo, and Lyle had a trio at the start of *Guys and Dolls* called "Fugue for Tinhorns." It's three gamblers boasting about the horses they're betting on, sung like a round, with voices overlapping. We got to hear it at the start of rehearsal one evening. Morales stood up in front of the whole cast and said this number set the tone for the whole show. He wanted us to watch it and catch the mood.

As they sang, I looked at James and Theo. One tall and blond, undeniably Timberlakian. The other shorter and darker, suddenly stripped of all teenagery awkwardness—a gangster and a gambler with a hard edge and a thick Brooklyn accent. Theo became his character, Benny Southstreet.

Demi was sitting next to me. "Did you decide which one?" he whispered when they were done. "Because I vote for the tall blondie."

"That's because blonds are your type," I said.

"I don't have a type!"

"Oh, yeah?"

"I don't! I am open to a full half of the human race. Have you talked to him any more?"

"James? Not much. He sat with me and Iz the other day at breakfast, but I was scared of being late for Acting, so I cut out early."

"Well, there's my answer," said Demi.

"What?"

"You like the other one."

"Shut up!"

"You do. I can see it."

"Don't talk about it with Blake and Lyle, okay?" I said. "It's not gonna go anywhere."

"You underestimate your gawky-sexy powers, my darling Sadye. I bet if you flutter those eyelashes, that short Asian boy will be all over you like a dog."

"I think we're just friends."

"That's your choice," said Demi.

THE NEXT NIGHT we ran *Guys and Dolls* as a company for the first time. During Lyle's show-stopping number, "Sit Down, You're Rockin' the Boat," Morales hopped up and gave Lyle three gestures—arm movements that fused the Nicely-Nicely Johnson gangster persona and the gospel revival flavor of the song he was singing. Almost like magic, the number turned from a pleasant tune into a rollicking celebration.

When Lyle finished, Morales called out to him. "I want you to add something in for me. Give me that fat man jiggle, the belly, the whole thing."

And Lyle did it, rolling and jiggling his round body across the stage in an unbelievable expression of ecstasy and delight. It was hilarious. But I could just see him register those words as Morales gave him the direction. Like "Oh, I'm nothing but the fat man now. I'm only seventeen, but this is my box, and I guess I've got to stay in it."

I don't think you call someone fat like that. Even if he is. Fat.

It wasn't just Lyle. We all jumped when Morales said "Jump." Like puppets. Not like people. He was so good at what he did, and at the same time so uninterested in communicating with the actors, hearing our ideas, considering our feelings, or doing anything but getting his singular vision onto the stage.

He didn't even remember my name; called me "Tall Hot Box," which made me cringe. But I watched him with total attention—shifting tiny pieces into place; making a joke funny, reblocking a scene to give it more energy, demanding absolute perfection and total attention from every member of his cast.

I could see why people idolized him. He was the opposite of Reanne, who was so involved with her idea of process and ensemble that she failed to step back and see the big picture. Reanne was kind and quite interesting to talk to, but she was translating Shakespeare's poetry into a muddle onstage.

Morales was bossy, decisive, and visionary. He was looking for results, and he expected professionalism from everyone. He wasn't thinking about the actors and their inner lives at all. He was thinking about the audience. He wanted us to deliver what he needed as a director as quickly and seamlessly as possible—whereas Reanne wanted us to search inside ourselves for truths and then translate those to stage gestures that felt organic.

I wasn't sure who was right.

Maybe Reanne was right in her philosophy but also a bad director. Which would mean Morales was wrong but also good.

MISS ADELAIDE was the best part in *Guys and Dolls*, and Nanette wasn't typecast for it. Her Adelaide glittered with freshness, at least to anyone who'd seen the movie or listened to the cast album. Usually small, childish, and sharp-looking, in this show Nanette was bawdy and pushing forty. Her edge became Adelaide's hard-spent years on the nightclub circuit. Her tiny figure became a surprising ball of fury when she yelled at her gambler fiancé. She had a Broadway voice and the experience to do whatever Morales asked of her the first time he asked.

It wasn't fair.

We were jealous. All the Hot Box Girls. Not just because she had what we wanted. But because she deserved it.

(shuffle, click)

Sadye: I'm here in wardrobe with the Hot Box Girls: Iz, Jade, Kirsten, Bec, and Dawn. Say hello, ladies.

Ladies: Hello!

Bec: Hello, Sadye's recorder thing.

Sadye: We're doing second fittings for 'Mink' costumes. They put Velcro down the sides of the gowns so we can rip them off, and now we're making sure they work.

Jade: Mine wouldn't come undone, I don't know, I got mighty-Velcro.

Sadye: Nanette got fitted first, so she's gone back to class. The rest of us are missing Pantomime, or whatever.

Iz: They're fixing Jade's dress right now.

Sadye: Dawn, tell posterity what we're wearing.

Dawn: Okay. Um. Black tights, character shoes, slips covered with gold sequins.

Kirsten: It's what we wear under the evening gowns.

Jade: Red garters, don't forget, red garters.

Sadye: And wigs! We all have black wigs.

Iz: For "Bushel and a Peck" we're redheads, right?

Jade: Yeah, that's what they picked. And Nanette will be white blonde.

Dawn: Did you see her wig?

Bec: Yeah, didn't you?

Jade: Why does Nanette get to be platinum? I want to be platinum!

Kirsten: Because Nanette gets everything.

Dawn: Because she's Nanette.

Jade: Maybe someone will shoot her.

Sadye: Or maybe she'll get sick and go home.

Dawn: I'm her understudy. I can't shoot her, or they'll be suspicious. Bec, you should do it.

Bec: Maybe I'll poison her lemonade.

Kirsten: Oh, that lemonade, all the time. "I have to drink lemonade for my throat. Do you mind if I just get some lemonade?" Uggh.

Dawn: Did you hear her telling Morales about what her *Annie* director said? *Annie, Annie, Annie*--if I hear any more about that stupid touring production, I'm gonna barf.

Sadye: She was only the understudy.

Dawn: No!

Sadye: Yes. She makes it seem like she was the lead, but most of the time she was just an orphan. Iz, back me up.

Iz: It's true.

Dawn: Oh, that is so rich.

Kirsten: I'm in *Showboat* with her, too, and I'm sorry, but that girl has got to rein in her attitude.

Sadye: What bothers me is that she's here, competing with students. She's been on Broadway

already. Can't she give someone
else a chance?

Iz: *(annoyed)* This isn't elementary
school, Sadye. It's not about
everybody getting a turn.

Sadye: I know.

Iz: It's about talent. People who
have talent get what they
deserve. That's how it is in
theater.

Sadye: What are you saying, then?

Iz: Nothing. I'm not talking about
you.

Jade: Ooh! You guys, check me out
in this fringe thing.

(shuffle, click)

I KNEW IZ hadn't meant it the way it sounded. But it
hurt just the same.

THAT NIGHT, after Hot Box rehearsal was over, I
stopped to buy a candy bar from the vending
machine outside the studios, letting the other girls go
on ahead.

"Hey, Peter Quince." It was Theo.

"Don't call me that, ugh!" I said it playfully.

"Sorry. How about Tall Hot Box?"

"I hate how he still doesn't know my name."

"He doesn't know mine, either," Theo said, falling into step with me as I headed down the path. Theo had the front of his hoodie zipped all the way to the top, and he walked with a comical spring to his step. I liked that about him. I was suddenly conscious of the sweat that had dried into my leotard and soaked into my hair. I had talked big about the sweaty French-fry pounce, but now that it seemed like a possibility, I had my doubts.

"You, um. You looked amazing doing that, that mink dance yesterday," Theo mumbled.

"Oh, thanks."

"Yeah. I, ah, I hadn't seen it before."

"'Fugue for Tinhorns' was great," I told him. "It's gonna be a phenomenal opening." I kept talking, babbling about the show, when I realized Theo was looking at me, in the light of the streetlamps on the path. There was no one else around. He was staring, with his eyes all soft, like the mink dance had done something to him.

Theo had re-noticed me.

Okay, forget the sweat. It was clearly time to

pounce. I grabbed Theo's elbow flirtatiously, leaning into him while we talked about what our costumes were going to be. I could feel the hard muscles of his arm through the cotton of his hoodie.

"Demi told me they fitted him for a lilac suit," I said. "And a light-blue one. Did you have costume fittings yet?"

"They're going against type." Theo nodded. "All the gangsters will be in white, cream, and tan. With Demi in blue and purple, and Sam in shades of green."

"Ooh, swank," I said. "But Demi is having a hissy fit because he looks washed out in lilac," I said. "He thinks it makes his skin look ashy."

"He'll be fine. Your friend Demi's good, I gotta give him that," Theo said.

"He gets up there and light bursts out of him."

"Well, I wouldn't have said that, exactly, but yeah."

"He was in a boys choir when he was little. That's where he learned to sing."

Theo looked at me carefully. "You two are close, aren't you?"

"He's the most talented person I know."

We were outside the boys' dorm. Theo stopped and looked at me, his hands in the pockets of his jeans. "Well, I guess it's good night, then," he said quietly.

Okay, pounce again. I took a step toward him. Standing too close.

I mean, I thought I had a right to hope, after what he said about the mink dance. After the soft staring he'd been doing in the light from the streetlamps.

But he didn't kiss me. Or do anything. He just gave a little wave and took off into the dorm at a run.

In THE TECH rehearsal, Morales had decided at the last minute that the yellow-feathered dresses the Hot Box girls wore during "A Bushel and a Peck" weren't funny enough, and reduced the costume mistress to tears by demanding seven chicken hats in two hours.

"What do you mean, a chicken hat?" she had shouted at him, coming out from the wings and standing near the edge of the stage.

"A hat with the head of a chicken on it!" he bellowed. "A big chicken. Use those chickens from the *Our Town* set last year. You can find them. The girls need to look like sexy, sexy chickens, or this number will go in the toilet! And while you're at it, get Nanette a farm girl dress instead of this shorts thing."

"So you want six chicken hats, then, because you're keeping Nanette in farmer clothes? Six, not seven?"

"No. Give me seven, in case. Seven of everything. I might want Nanette to be a chicken, too."

The costume mistress crossed her arms, squinting in the harsh stage lighting while Morales sat in the audience. "This is not what we discussed, Jacob."

"No, it is not," he said. "But this is what we're doing."

She stomped away, furiously wiping her eyes, and disappeared through a side door.

But within an hour and a half, Morales got his hats. Nanette got a new outfit. And ridiculous as it sounds, they made the number better. Morales was like a mean magician—everyone he touched quivered in fear, but they were all transformed once he turned his attention to them.

After tech we ran the first half of the show, and after "Bushel and a Peck," Morales announced he was calling in some singers to augment the sound of the Hot Box Girls from backstage. Two altos and two sopranos would learn the song tomorrow morning and sing with us at the dress rehearsal.

As we all dispersed, the music director beckoned me over. "Sadye, I hate to ask you this, but when the new voices come in tomorrow, I'm going to want you to lip-synch."

"What?"

"Lip-synch. You're throwing off the harmonies, sweetie. You have a tendency to go flat."

"Can't you teach me?" I asked. "Can't you show me where I should put my voice? Some of these girls have had years of singing lessons."

He shook his head. "I could teach you. Probably I could," he said. "But not in time for opening. Not in time for this show."

"But I want to sing!" I cried, suddenly close to tears. "I'm trying."

He stood up and shrugged into his jacket. "There's only one thing to want in this situation, sweetie. You need to want what's best for the show."

"I love this show," I said to him. And I meant it.

"Okay, then," he said. "What are you going to do if you love the show?"

I sighed. "I'm going to stay silent."

"Good girl." He chucked me under the chin and gestured for Demi and Candie to come up to the piano.

I WALKED BACK to the dorms alone that night, maybe ten steps behind the rest of the dancers.

Thinking. About how I couldn't sing.

I could get better, sure. But if I wasn't good enough to sing Hot Box Girl harmonies, it was a decent bet I'd never be good enough to sing a solo, much less carry a lead role.

"Show what Sadye can do"—that's what Demi had told me. But it was becoming increasingly clear that what Sadye could do was *less* than what a lot of other people could.

Was I good enough to be at Wildewood?

What would I do if I wasn't good enough?

What would I do?

Who would I be?

"Hey there, Sadye!" It was Nanette, coming down the path alone. The last person I wanted to see just then. Her with her big voice and her two leading roles and her "perfect, sweetie" self.

But Nanette looked so small, and so lonely, walking in the dark. So I said, "Hey, darling," and sat down on one of the benches that lined the path.

Nanette joined me. "Let me ask you something."

"Sure."

"I know they're all talking about me," she said. "They are, right?"

"Who?"

"The Hot Box Girls. Maybe not you and Iz, but Jade and the rest of them."

"What? No." I lied.

"Be honest. They hate my guts, I can feel it."

Of course it was true. I had done it myself, though nothing as bad as Bec, Dawn, and Kirsten. "Child can't tap to save her life, she's barely getting through the routine." "She can't fill out her evening dress, I don't know how that's supposed to be sexy." "Little Miss Perfect, thinks she's better than a chocolate cupcake." "Her and her lemonade." "Her and her *Annie*." "Ugh."

Thing was, I did like Nanette. For all her pretensions and her attitude, I could see she worked harder than anyone else and I admired her talent. Plus, she made me laugh. But I had never told any of the girls to shut up, and it was me who told them she was the understudy in *Annie*.

Not only that, I'd said I wished she'd stayed home. I even had it on tape.

Now, looking at her determined jaw quivering as if she were about to cry, I felt like a monster. "They're just jealous," I said to her. "We're all jealous. We can't help it."

"So they *are* talking about me?"

I nodded. "It's the situation. They'd talk about anyone who was Adelaide."

Nanette sighed. "It was like that in *Annie*, too," she said. "The girl who played the lead? Jenny Forsythe. We all hated her. We'd get quiet whenever she walked in the dressing room, and we'd all go to the mall without her on the days off. Then she got bronchitis for three weeks and I had to step in, and it was like the other girls suddenly hated me instead. I was so relieved when she came back, but it took a while before they were nice to me again."

"Um, Nanette?"

"What?"

"Maybe it would help if you didn't talk so much about *Annie* and *Fiddler* and stuff."

"What?"

"You talk about them, like, all the time."

"But it's my life. Everyone seems to think it's interesting."

"It *is* interesting. But it also makes us kinda sick."

"Oh."

"Yeah."

Nanette reached down, untied her shoe, and retied it. "Is this what school is like?"

"You mean with the girls talking about each other?"

"Uh-huh."

"I don't have any girlfriends at school," I said. "Not really. I only have Demi."

"Well, that's more than I've got."

* * *

IN *Bye Bye Birdie*, which Demi and Iz rehearsed in the afternoons, there is a put-upon dad character whose shining moment comes when he and his family get to be on *The Ed Sullivan Show*, which was a TV show like *David Letterman*, but even bigger. The dad is so, so excited to be on the show that he sings this song called "Hymn for a Sunday Evening," which basically has only one lyric—"Ed Sullivan"—sung like it's a religious epiphany. A chorus comes in behind him like a choir of angels, and he's just ecstatic.

Anyway. When not immersed in *Guys and Dolls* or *Bye Bye Birdie*, Demi was as excited over Buff Blond Blake from Boston as this dad was over Ed Sullivan. And he'd sing, to the same tune:

Blake Polacheck!
Blake Polacheck!
I wanna be on
Blake Polacheck!
Blake! Blake!
Pol! Pol!
Someday we'll recall,
The greatest lay of all!
Blake Pooooooool-a-cheeeeeeek!

So long as Blake wasn't present.

And he wasn't present, not often. I'd estimate he kissed Demi twice more in the days leading up to the *Guys and Dolls* performance. Most of the time he was elusive—always running somewhere after class, rushing off to take a shower, going to meet someone he'd promised to hang with.

To anyone with even a moderate amount of experience, or even to me, it was obvious Blake wasn't that interested. He could have his pick of any guy or girl at Wildewood, and he clearly found Demi cute enough but too flamboyant, or maybe just too much *person*.

Whatever. Only someone who's lived his entire romantic life in his dreams could fail to see that Blake was not signing up for the role of Blond Boyfriend, and that he was sending "back off" messages whenever he wasn't licking Demi's neck.

But Demi didn't see it. And when I told him, he said, "You don't know what it's like when we're alone, darling"—and what can you say to that?

On the Friday of the ten-day wonder dress rehearsal, I walked to lunch with Blake and Demi. We all had Pantomime in the same building, though with different teachers.

Demi was bouncing along, talking about *Guys and Dolls*, so in his element, so pleased with himself, a hundred thousand times happier than I'd ever seen him in Ohio. And Blake said, "Dude, I gotta meet someone. I'm gonna skip lunch. I'll catch you guys later," and ran off toward the dorms.

We went to lunch and then back to Demi's room for the twenty minutes before class, since he had a box of chocolates there from his parents, who were still on their European tour/safari and not coming to see the show.

We walked in, and there was Blake on Demi's low bunk, making out with Mark.

They had their clothes on. But still. Demi took one look at them and bolted through the door. I could hear his footsteps down the hall and out.

Blake and Mark lay there, looking at me. "Do you mind?" Blake finally said.

As if it were his room. As if it weren't Demi's bed. As if he didn't know me.

"I need to get the chocolate," I answered, keeping my ground.

"S'over there," said Mark, pointing to the top of Demi's dresser. "It's Godiva."

"Those are the best," said Blake, stretching himself out flirtatiously on the bunk.

I grabbed the box and left.

* * *

DEMI WAS waiting for me outside. I put my arm around him and we walked down to the lakeshore. I opened the chocolates (it was a large box), and we sat silently in the sand, poking the bottoms with our fingernails until we found the ones we liked best.

Demi ate two at a time, like he wanted to flood himself with some sensation other than what he was feeling about Blake and Mark.

Finally, he said, "I'm thirsty."

"Me too. Chocolate does that."

"Hm."

"We can stop at the lounge on the way back and get sodas."

"Okay." Demi poked his thumb into the bottom of a strawberry cream. "Are we late for rehearsal?"

"We've got five minutes."

"How could he do that to me when I have a show? With Mark, Mark who I have to sleep underneath in that stupid bunk bed."

"I know."

"Ugh, they were on my *bed* even, how gross is that?"

"Very."

"I feel like, oh, like a discarded napkin."

"You're so much more than a napkin, darling."

"No, I'm a napkin. I've gone from top Bunburyer to limp, dirty old napkin in the course of an afternoon."

I patted him on the shoulder and offered him another chocolate.

"What should I do? Do I talk to him? Let it all hang out and like, cleanse my system of all this badness, or do I pretend like it never happened?"

"You pretend like it never happened," I said. "You keep your dignity."

"Ugh," Demi cried. "Why Mark? Why *Mark*? I mean, that guy doesn't even know how to flush a toilet."

"He's a jerk, Demi. Blake is a jerk."

"But even so, why would he pick Mark over me? Why?"

"There's no why. It sucks."

"I can't do the show tonight. Or tomorrow." Demi stood up decisively, wiping his eyes. "I'm going to have to tell Morales I can't go on. I'm never going to make it through, seeing Blake and Mark onstage, knowing they were Bunburying behind my back."

"Yes, you will."

"No, I can't do it. I'm going to crack, forget my lines, my throat will close up. It would be more professional to admit that and step down. Let the understudy do it."

"You can't be serious."

"Look at me!" he shouted. "I'm a napkin! That boy has reduced me to a napkin!"

"Demi." I stood up and grabbed his arm.

"What? You don't know how I feel just now, Sadye. Like I'm limp. I'm dizzy. I feel like I'm going to throw up," he yelled. "I'm not fit to do *anything*, much less sing and dance like freaking Elvis Presley, which I have to do all afternoon, then sing selections from *Porgy and Bess* for M-TAP, and then put on a lilac suit and be slick and romantic, singing full-out high notes and kissing Candie Berkolee, which is exactly what I'm scheduled to do. And my throat hurts now, I can't have my throat hurting, I won't be able to do it. Sadye, I'm so freaking tired, and I can't believe he did this to me, and I can't believe what I've got to do today, it's not possible, just no way I can do it, don't you see?"

"Demi! Demi!"

"My throat hurts! What?"

"Stop it. You have to stop it. Deep breathe!"

He didn't deep breathe, but he looked at me quietly.

"You can't drop *Guys and Dolls* because of Blake," I told him. "You can't. Look. Blake Bunburied with Mark because . . . Mark sucks. He's only halfway decent looking, he's not even funny, and you told me yourself he can barely remember his lines. Blake *wanted* someone mediocre. Otherwise he'd never pick Mark over you."

"What?" Demi obviously never read women's magazines. "Why?"

"People like mediocrity because it makes them feel better about themselves. He was intimidated by you," I went on. "Because Blake may be king of the cuteocracy, yes, he probably is—but *you*, you are king of the meritocracy. A guy like Blake doesn't want to play second string. He's used to being, like, the captain of sports teams and always getting his way. So think about their mediocrity, when you get onstage tonight. Think, 'There you are, two untalented dudes with shaky ethical foundations.' Think, 'There you two dudes are, dressed as policemen in the wings, and here am I, singing "Luck Be a Lady" center stage.' Think, 'I am king of the meritocracy, and your afternoon make-out sessions are nothing to me because Broadway is my next stop and you two are gonna be eating my dust!'" I was shouting now, holding Demi's hand.

He finally smiled. Then he hugged me tight. "Thanks, Sadye."

"Of course."

He kept hugging me, like he had forgotten what we were doing and started thinking about something else. I could feel his mind begin to regroup and race on. "You're gonna be late for rehearsal if you don't leave now," I whispered in his ear.

"Oh, no! Is it one already?" Demi released me and bent down to pick up the chocolate box. "I gotta move. You're the best, Sadye. I love you. The most incredible girl."

"That's what they tell me," I said.

He ran off at top speed, holding the gold box on his head with one hand.

(click)

> **Sadye:** Hello, posterity. I'm on the beach, after lunch. Demi just ran off to *Birdie* rehearsal, but I'm avoiding *Midsummer*.
>
> I know Reanne is waiting for me. And it's rude and destructive to be late, because it destroys the spirit of the ensemble. But I hate the show.
>
> I hate being a tree, I hate being a man, and I hate the way Reanne is pushing people to embody the spirit of whatever in the forest when it's clear that Titania, for example, has no idea what

the heck she's saying. She
doesn't know what her speeches
even mean, but Reanne isn't
going to tell her because she's
encouraging the spirit of
discovery and empowering the
actor. Except I doubt Titania is
ever going to figure it out, and
she's going to go up there in
performance and just speak in
this vague fairy way, and no
one is going to know what's
going on.

The set design is junky and
distracting to the audience.
Yesterday we began "canvas work"
and spent half the rehearsal
experimenting with wrapping
ourselves up in this bright
green canvas to look like trees.

And add to that, we're all wearing
unitards. Reanne announced--and
can I just say she actually
seemed happy about this?--that
there were extra unitards left
over from the order they'd
placed for *Cats*, and our
production was going to have

brand-new, shiny black unitards
to wear. I guess she thought
we'd be glad to have something
new, since most of the
productions use costumes from
the shop's collection that get
reworked, rather than built from
scratch.

Think about it.

Lyle. In a unitard.

Me, in a unitard, playing a man.

No one wants to wear them.

How is anyone going to tell the
fairies from the mechanicals? Or
from the *trees*? There are so
many amazing ways you could
dress the lovers--one couple in
reds, another in blue--one
conservative, another goth--one
Elizabethan, another modern
day--and instead we're going to
have trouble telling brunette
Helena from brunette Hermia in
unitards.

I wanted to talk to Demi about it,
but he's all freaked about *Guys
and Dolls* and Blake messing
around with Mark and--I can't

bring it up with him until after
tonight.
And now I am late. Right this
minute. On purpose.
Because it's one thing to be
committed when you believe in
what you're doing. But what are
you supposed to do when you
don't believe?
(shuffle, shuffle, click)

I SPOKE UP. In *Midsummer* rehearsal. And while in
hindsight I should have arranged to talk to Reanne pri-
vately about my staging ideas and the deadening confusion of the tree spirit thing we were all doing, I didn't. I
let myself get irritated after twenty-five minutes of
standing with my arms out, trying to keep an expression of bemused wonder on my face as the principals
rehearsed.

"Reanne?" I said, when she stopped the lovers to
fine-tune some blocking. "Starveling and Snug and me
shouldn't have to be trees while we do this. It's gonna
take forever and our arms are gonna snap off."

Snug and Starveling put their arms down by
their sides when I spoke, but they didn't say anything.

Reanne took a few steps toward me. "Sadye, are you telling me how to direct this rehearsal?"

And you know what? I was.

I was mad about being a tree, yes. I admit that was part of it. But Starveling looked close to fainting, and I felt it was time to speak up—not just about how uncomfortable everyone was on tree duty, and how humiliating it was to stand around there and basically be furniture, but also about the way it was going to look onstage.

Yeah, everyone kept telling me a good actor should commit fully and not undermine the director's vision— but most of these people were goofing around and making jokes and hadn't even learned their lines. I was the only one who even cared enough about the show to do anything about the fact that the trees sucked, and morale was down, and the show was falling apart. So in a way, I was more committed than any of them.

"The trees aren't working," I said. "They're distracting from the scenes, no matter how good a job people try to do."

A few of the actors nodded.

"Really, if you sit there and watch the scenes, which I've done when I'm not a tree, people are moving unintentionally. And they look tired, or bored, which takes away from the action. Plus, it's really hard to believe they're trees because they're *way* too short."

"Especially me," quipped Snug, and Starveling laughed.

"Maybe we should have some actual trees built of cardboard or wire, instead of people," I went on. "Or what if—what if we weren't so literal, and had a set that wasn't a forest but like an interpretation of a forest. Like a forest entirely of roses?"

Reanne raised her eyebrows.

"Or a city. A city that was like an urban jungle of dark corners and streetlamps instead of trees. Or what if it felt like we were underwater somehow? So it would feel less pedestrian. Like an underwater wonderland, like we'd all fallen into a magical ocean." I knew I was babbling, but the ideas spilled out of me.

"Sadye," said Reanne, her voice sounding almost sad. "Can we please continue the rehearsal?"

I liked Reanne. I did. And I could tell that she thought I'd been horrible and obnoxious just then. So I nodded and put my arms out like a tree.

But I felt sure I was right.

AFTER REHEARSAL, Lyle, Theo, and Starveling walked with me to Restoration Squash-your-boobs-up.

"That was very Peter Quince of you," Lyle said,

putting his arm around me. "And I mean that in the nicest possible way."

"How 'Peter Quince'?"

"You know, he's the director, he's trying to make all these layabouts behave themselves and put on a decent play. But they're out of his control."

"Oh."

"You fought the good fight," said Theo. "Even if she didn't want to hear it. I like the underwater idea."

Lyle shook his head. "Oh, no you don't. I personally veto the underwater idea."

"Why?"

"It's enough I have to wear a donkey head. No way am I wearing a bathing suit. That's worse than the unitards!"

"Oh, come on," I said. "We could all wear period bathing suits, like 1940s ones so we'd look like Esther Williams."

"Excuse me, Madame With the Ideas," said Lyle. "I'm like Winona Ryder. I insist on the no-nudity clause. The forest of roses idea was better."

"Thank you. I like that one myself."

"Were you, like, thinking of those in advance?" asked Starveling.

"Not exactly," I said. "I didn't plan to tell them to

Reanne. They popped out. But I had to think of something while I was on tree duty."

"Wow," said Starveling. "I think about sex."

"Is that why you're always about to faint?"

"Maybe. Probably, yeah."

Lyle squeezed my shoulder. "You know she's never
gonna do any of those, right?"

"Yeah. I know it."

"I'm gonna drink some orange juice before
rehearsal tomorrow," said Starveling. "I really almost
fainted this time."

MY PARENTS drove up from Brenton the next night
to watch *Guys and Dolls*. I saw them for an hour before
the show—they came to dinner in the cafeteria. My dad
brought me a bouquet of flowers, limp from the long
car ride.

There wasn't much to say, somehow. Demi sat with
us, since he had no family there to see him—and I realized, thinking about Brenton for practically the first
time since we'd arrived at Wildewood, that I hadn't seen
Demi's straight-boy drag since we left Ohio. Not that he
used it with my parents anymore, anyway—but all ves-
tiges of it had disappeared.

He took one of my roses and put it behind his ear for the entire meal. Then the adults got coffee and we had to leave for our call.

"Break a leg!" my mother said, signing at the same time. "Break two legs!"

"Thank you!" said Demi. "I didn't know you knew that phrase."

"It's the right thing to say, isn't it?" she asked. "My friend at work told me."

"Absolutely, Mrs. Paulson."

"Okay, so break them!" she said. "Go, go!"

We went.

T HE SHOW was fantastic.

Demi was dashing and manly and utterly convincing as the tough guy brought low by his love for the good-hearted mission worker. He had been a little off in dress rehearsal the night before, but in performance he didn't choke, or lose his voice, or betray his broken heart in any way except that he sang with so much emotion I believed every note. Candie was wounded and gentle at the same time: her Sarah was a woman with a heart so big she didn't know what to do with all her feelings about the world, so she worked for charity and squelched her personal life so her passions wouldn't overwhelm her. Nanette was brassy and tough and falling apart underneath. We all looked sexy-ridiculous in our chicken hats. And Lyle brought the show to a halt with his fat man dance and his eleven o'clock number "Sit Down, You're Rockin' the Boat."

He had to reprise it three times before the audience let the show go on.

It was so different doing it in performance. With people responding. Looking up and laughing. Clapping after the songs. Seeing my parents smiling in the middle of the second row.

In dress rehearsal, *Guys and Dolls* had seemed good and clever and bright—but with an audience it became buoyant. Glittering.

There were six curtain calls. And I thought: I have to find some way to stay in this world.

I CHANGED MY clothes, said good-bye to my parents, and headed over to the cast party in the black box theater. Curfew was extended. I started out dancing with Demi and Lyle (as far away from Blake and Mark as we could get), then with Iz and Candie, then with Nanette, then with the other Hot Box Girls, and suddenly, someone put his hands over my eyes.

Theo?

No. James. "You were great tonight," he said.

Covered in butter, I thought.

Theo ran away without kissing me, but James is covered in butter.

"You were, too," I said, smiling up at him. Which is rare—when there's a guy I can smile up at.

"And you look fantastic."

"Six pounds of makeup will do that to a girl."

"No, it's not that," James said. "Hey, you wanna get some fresh air?"

I looked around. It was Theo I wanted, but all the evidence suggested I didn't have a chance. I couldn't even see him anywhere. "Sure."

We stepped out into the muggy summer night, and James started walking. "Where are you going?" I laughed.

"I don't know," James answered. "Walk with me."

But he did know. We went right down to the beach. The site of "several midnight debaucheries resulting in expulsion," according to Lyle.

We took off our shoes and waded into the water, chatting about the show.

Then James took off his shirt and plunged in.

He had a good body. Here he was, doing something close to a jumbo-pounce. So I thought, why not?

I'm not Sarah with Lurking Bigness anymore. I'm Sadye, who is Big already. Sadye, who just performed in the most awesome show. Sadye, who is living the way she wants to.

I thanked the goddess Liza Minnelli that I was wearing a bra that matched my underpants, pulled off my dress, and went swimming.

James swam up to meet me, and before I knew it, we were kissing. I had never in my whole life kissed a boy with just my underwear on. In fact, I'd only kissed one boy ever in ninth grade. And now, here was boy with a bare chest. His braces were clunky, but his mouth was soft, and we were floating, and the water made us slippery. "I've been looking at you for a long time," he whispered. "Have you been looking at me?"

"Yes," I answered, lying a little.

We kissed some more, and part of me was thinking that this felt amazing, that this was what I wanted—but part of me was thinking this wasn't the right boy. It was all moving too fast.

"I'm cold," I said, pulling back.

"Let me keep you warm."

It sounded like such a line.

I didn't want a guy to keep me warm. I wanted a guy to make me laugh and play songs on the piano for me and debate me and tease me and *then* keep me warm. James and I weren't at the keeping-warm stage.

I splashed up onto shore, shivering, and pulled my dress on over my wet underwear.

"Sadye, wait!" James followed me out of the water. "What's up?"

"I'm just cold," I said. "I think I want to go to bed."

That sounded wrong.

"I mean, you're great and all, I just—I just want to go home on my own, okay?

"Hey," he said, pulling on his dry shirt and shaking his hair around to get the water out of it. "I didn't mean to be pushy. You—you took off all your clothes."

"I know," I said. "I changed my mind."

"Fine."

"I know it's probably not," I said, putting on my sandals. "I know I'm being a jerk."

"No, it's fine, really. Whatever."

"Okay, then. Good night."

"See ya."

I left him standing by the shore, but I didn't go back to the dorm right away. Instead, I went back to the party, my clothes damp and my hair wet, and I danced the rest of the night with Demi.

Theo turned up later, holding hands with Bec.

* * *

IN ACTING CLASS, we began doing monologues. A couple days after *Guys and Dolls* performed, I had to stand up and recite a speech from *Medea*. When I finished, Morales brought the entire group around to look at the way my foot had tensed while I'd been speaking. My toes were curled under, he pointed out.

Then he gave a long lecture on leaving our personal *agita*, our tics and pains—and in essence, our personalities—behind as we stood up onstage. People nodded and looked at my foot like it was some festering disease that they didn't want to catch.

"What if we want to bring our personalities with us?" I asked Morales. "Isn't that what people do who are method actors? Stanislavski and Strasberg and all that?"

I had read about the Method in a book, before coming to Wildewood. I had figured that since I had no acting training, I should study up on it so I wouldn't be behind. Basically, the idea is that method actors don't try to act like different characters. They try to be themselves and just respond to what is happening. They draw on their own personal memories and experiences rather than inventing ones for their characters, and they speak and gesture as naturally as possible.

"Method is for film acting," said Morales dismissively. "That's not what you're learning here."

"But there have been method actors on the stage," I persisted. "What about Marlon Brando?"

Morales snorted. "You, whatever your name is. You cannot argue out of the fact that you have a tense foot. You have tensed this foot all through your monologue for a week now. Forget the Method. Forget Marlon Brando."

"Why?"

"You are not Brando, and you're not going to reinvent basic dramatic technique by arguing with me. Just attempt to learn what I am teaching. Do not try to be Brando. The man is dead, anyhow."

"I—" I struggled to find the right words. "I'm not saying I did a good job with *Medea*, or anything. I'm not trying to say I know what I'm doing. I'm trying to have a conversation about acting. About what it means to be an actor. Aren't there different methods we should have at our disposal?"

"Get your foot uncurled and maybe we can talk about it," said Morales. But he didn't ask me to do the scene again.

(click, shuffle, bang, bang)
    Demi: Is it on?
    Sadye: Wait. Wait. Yeah. Okay,
        go.

Demi: It's July ninth--

Sadye: No, it's the tenth--

Demi: It is? sorry. No idea what day it is here.

Sadye: --and we're recording our impressions of Wildewood at a little more than two weeks in.

Demi: Oh, let's sing the Blake song. We need to lay that down for posterity.

Sadye: Okay.

Demi: Sadye wrote me a Blake song, more of a rhyme, really, to be like an exorcism.

Sadye: To get Blake out of his system.

Demi: And it is working, can I just say? I heartily recommend the nasty Paulson rhyme method of recovering from heartbreak. Ready?

Sadye: Ready.

Demi: Five, six, seven, eight!

Together: Blechy, blondy,

Blake the buff,

Looking good

Is not enough.

You can smile

And bat your eye,

Shake your butt

And flash your thigh.

But until

Your IQ's high,

You will never

Be my guy!

(self-congratulatory clapping)

Demi: Oh, that makes me feel so much better! I don't know what I ever saw in him.

Sadye: Muscles?

Demi: Besides muscles.

Sadye: Just call me Love Doctor.

Demi: Love Doctor! All right. Now, for posterity's sake, give us your report. Acting, Singing, Restoration-Squash-your-boobs-up, Combat-with-hunky-straight-boys, *Midsummer Night's Disaster*-- whatever you have to share.

Sadye: In Acting we are learning, like, the anti-Method.

Demi: You don't think Morales is brilliant?

Sadye: I don't know. I thought he was. He might still be. But do you think he should be telling people who are only seventeen that they're not Brando?

Demi: Oh, you're mad about the tense-foot lecture. That was mean, I give you that.

Sadye: He acts like he can see exactly what we're worth and that's the end of it. But who's to say that's the case?

Demi: He is a Broadway director.

Sadye: Yeah, but we're not even out of school and he's got everyone pegged already.

Demi: And?

Sadye: I mean, of course I'm not Brando, because Brando was Brando. I know that. I'm not trying to say I'm a genius. I mean, I basically suck at the moment. But the point is, I *could* be Brando. I mean, I could be Brando*ish*. Is he so sure by looking at me that I'm not?

Demi: Sadye--

Sadye: Maybe I have Lurking Brandoishness that would explode onto the stage if only my acting teacher weren't humiliating me

by having everyone stare at my
feet?

Demi: He's teaching us to take
direction.

Sadye: Why should I forget the
Method if I think it's
interesting? Lots of great
actors have used it. Don't you
remember that book I had on it?

Demi: Part of his point is that if
you can't take the heat in his
class, you won't be able to take
the heat in the real world.

Sadye: But don't you think there
should be a dialogue? Not just
him yelling at me, but more like
a conversation about what we're
trying to learn?

Demi: There are twenty people in
that class, Sadye. Not just you.

Sadye: Yes, but they're like
sheep. Like acting sheep who do
whatever he tells them to do.

Demi: I don't think of it that
way.

Sadye: Then how do you think about
it?

Demi: Like learning from a master.

Sadye: *(pause)* We should change the subject or we'll have our Second Official Quarrel.

Demi: Fine. *(another pause)* I had a first costume fitting today. For *Birdie*.

Sadye: You did?

Demi: Yes. And I have one word for you.

Sadye: What?

Demi: Gold lamé.

Sadye: That's two words.

Demi: All right. Two words. But gold lamé. Tight, tight, gold lamé.

Sadye: Speaking of costumes, I have a word for you, too. For *Midsummer* costumes. Actually, I can't believe I haven't told you this yet.

Demi: What?

Sadye: Unitard.

Demi: Say it isn't so.

Sadye: Unitard. Unitard. Lyle didn't tell you?

Demi: I am sure Lyle doesn't want to think about it.

Sadye: Unitard. Unitard!

Demi: I love that word. *A*
    Midsummer Night's Unitard.
(click)

MIDSUMMER rehearsal, three weeks in. Reanne gave Titania this blocking to do that involved her circling me (the tree) in a relaxed, flirtatious fashion, the way someone might do with an actual tree that was round and not person-shaped—and Titania tried to do it, but she ended up feeling my boob by accident and then tripping twice over the balled-up bits of canvas at my feet, and the whole move seemed so wrong; it was an important speech, she was tripping and stumbling during it. I wasn't stable and so I moved by accident when she hung on me; and the fact that I was a person (and not a tree) was going to end up pulling focus from Titania.

So I interrupted. "Reanne," I said. "I'm going to distract everyone by accident, here," I said. "When she hangs on me, I'm going to wobble, and everyone's going to think I'm coming to life."

"Thanks, Sadye, but we want to show Titania's intimate connection to the magical forest here. That's the reason for the blocking choice," said Reanne.

"I'm sorry I grabbed your boob," said Titania.

"S'okay," I said. "That's not the point. I just think you're going to get caught in all this canvas, and I'm going to wobble, and no one's going to pay good attention to the drama going on with Bottom."

"Sadye," said Reanne gently. "We've just put this blocking in. If it doesn't work after we've done the scene several times, we can restage it. But for now, let's try to make it happen."

"Can't we try it without the trees?" I said. "Or what if the trees dance some kind of forest fairy dance and then left the stage so as not to steal focus? Like a scene-setting thing?"

"Looking at it from here, I don't think you're stealing focus, Sadye."

"What if we moved Bottom and Titania downstage, to bring the audience's attention closer to them? And maybe dress the trees in costumes, to make the distinction clearer between trees and characters?"

"Let's run it, okay, my dear? Give it a try."

I admit I rolled my eyes a bit when Titania stumbled again trying to swing herself around my trunk.

But honestly.

* * *

AFTER REHEARSAL, I was heading off to Stage Combat with some of the mechanicals when Reanne pulled me aside and asked me to stay. "I want to tell you, Sadye, that you're a more powerful person here than you realize."

"What?"

"You have a strong personality and a lot of magnetism. I know you're not too happy with your part, but I gave you that part because I thought you'd have the strength to stretch yourself in ways that not many actors can—and because you seemed to have the confidence to take on a part most other girls wouldn't want."

"Oh." I was flattered, but I didn't buy it. Honestly, I think they were short one boy, I was the tallest girl they had, and from my audition they knew I could at least speak Shakespearean English, if not actually act it.

"You have the power to make this production as good as it can be," Reanne was saying. "We're in your hands. But you also have the power to erode our work with your negativity."

"What do you mean?"

"The other mechanicals, Titania, their faith in our ensemble is being disrupted by your vocal lack of support for what we're doing. If you could embrace your part and the world we're trying to create, I'm sure the rest of them would follow your lead. People will follow you if you get on board, Sadye. But at the moment your interruptions and bad attitude are spreading like a cancer through this production, and I know you don't want that to happen. Do you want that to happen?"

"Of course not."

"Then please. Bring a positive headspace to the next rehearsal, and I'm sure you'll see the play begin to come together."

"Okay," I mumbled. "Sorry."

Reanne hugged me. She was a huggy woman. "You're more important than you know, Sadye."

I thanked her, and walked outside, heading toward my Stage Combat class.

I couldn't help but notice that I'd been told to shut up.

LATER THAT afternoon, I got out of Stage Combat and was walking to the cafeteria when I saw Demi and Lyle ahead of me on the path.

Demi reached over and took Lyle's hand. Just for a moment—squeezed it and dropped it. Then Lyle leaned over and whispered in Demi's ear, letting his hand touch the back of Demi's neck.

There was something between them. I could tell.

"What's up with you and Lyle?" I whispered to Demi while we were in line for tacos and Lyle had gone to get pasta salad.

"I should have told you, Sadye. I'm so sorry." Demi looked contrite.

"But what is it?"

He took a plate of tacos and put them on his tray. "I don't know what to say. It's only been a couple days."

"A couple days?"

"I should have told you. My bad."

"You wouldn't mess with Lyle, would you?" I said. "Not like, to get back at Blake?"

It popped out of my mouth, accusing without my intending to. Because Lyle looked so happy. In love.

Whatever was going on between them, it was a big deal to Lyle. That was certain.

"Sadye, what are you saying?" Demi stopped halfway to the soda machine and looked at me.

"I hope you're not messing with him, that's all."

"What?"

"I hope you're not messing with him."

"I heard you," Demi said under his breath as people milled around us. "I—where does that come from? No one said I was messing with anyone."

"I know, but—"

"Really. When have I ever messed with anyone? Tell me."

"I didn't mean it that way."

"How did you mean it, then? Because it sounds to me like you're saying I mess with people."

"I—" This was all going wrong.

"Whose side are you on, here?" Demi looked hostile. "Mine or Lyle's?"

"Yours. Yours. Of course, yours."

"Then act like it." Demi turned his back and went to sit with Lyle and Nanette.

DEMI AND LYLE fell in love. Real love, based on huge admiration for each other's talent, passion for the theater, and a hunger for affection, plus a true interest in what the other one had to say. They accepted each other's faults, and teased each other, and had occasional spats about stupid things, and made up. They found each other beautiful and adorable. They told each other secrets.

Within days they were an established couple, so clear in their connection that even Candie just accepted them as a pair. Lots of nights they held court on the roof of the boys' dorm. After rehearsal or evening rec, the two of them made the eighteen-minute beer run down to the convenience store off campus, then lay on the roof drinking and staring at the stars, while acolytes like me, Iz, and Nanette basked in the glow of their happiness.

Demi was at home with Lyle at Wildewood. More at home than he ever had been anywhere else in the world.

More at home than he'd been with his parents.

And more at home than he had been with me.

Gone was the straight-boy drag and the drab don't-notice-me clothes. And gone with them was the urgency of the Sadye/Demi connection, what we had when I was the only one who loved what he was really like.

Demi at Wildewood and Demi with Lyle was Demi freed from the half-closet he'd lived in since long before we met. It was Demi who knew who he was— without fear.

I tried not to be jealous.

I GOT BACK into Demi's good graces two days after our fight by writing a song. Made an early morning run down to Cumberland to buy notebook paper and a hot-pink pen, then wrote it out in nice handwriting and passed it to Demi after Acting.

> *Demi and Lyle,*
> *Yes, Lyle and Demi,*
> *Oh, they will be together*
> *In health and in phlegm-y.*
> *Lyle and Demi,*
> *Yes, Demi and Lyle,*
> *Although I must admit*
> *That their age is juvenile,*
> *Lyle and Demi,*
> *Yes, Demi and Lyle,*
> *Their bond is even stronger than*
> *A hungry crocodile!*
> *They love each other so,*
> *It's not just about the sex.*
> *Yes, their bond is so much stronger than*
> *Tyrannosaurus rex!*

All was forgiven. Our Second Official Quarrel was over.

Still, I think that was when I began to lose Demi.

* * *

In Acting one day, Morales separated us into four groups and gave each group a physical state we had to work with. "Abdominal pain" he said to one. "Alcohol stupor" to another. And "extreme exhaustion" to a third. But to my group of three girls, he said "pregnant."

Now, I've had abdominal pain. I've been exhausted, though maybe not extremely. And I'm sad to say I've been in an alcohol stupor, thanks to Demi's parents' open wine cabinet and our dumb attempt to be cosmopolitan while watching *Damn Yankees*. But I have never been pregnant, or known anyone pregnant, and it seemed to me a bit unfair.

But hey, actors have to portray emotions and situations they've never experienced, right? And the point of the exercise must be (I said to myself as I tried to walk around the room eight months pregnant) that afterward, Morales is going to give us techniques for pushing ourselves into mental and physical spaces we've never experienced.

But he didn't. Instead, he stopped us and made a few quick comments. "Demi, great commitment, but when we go next I'm going to ask you to pull it back a bit. A softer touch. Veronica, you're acting with your face but not your body. I want you to bring the body into it. And. Let me see." He walked over to me and snapped his fingers in my face. "What's your name, again, what is it? Quickly."

"Sadye," I told him. "I was in your show. And I'm not Marlon Brando. Remember?"

"You are supposed to be what? What are you supposed to be?"

"Pregnant."

"Then what are you giving me, this waddley thing you're doing? Show everyone what you were doing."

I did my pregnant lady walk as well as I could.

"Stop! Stop!" Morales cringed as if my acting were causing him physical pain. "Think about it from your feet. From your torso. Through your shoulders. Because right now, no one knows you are pregnant. The audience *does not know* she is pregnant!" he shouted. "Listen. Everyone, give me your complete attention, because this is important. When I am directing a play—when anyone is directing a play—it is your job as actors to give the director what he wants. You may not do it well, not yet. You may even do it badly, or he may want you to do it a different way than what you try at first. But you absolutely must deliver what he asks for. That is the skill of acting. If he wants you to be pregnant, give it to him. Then he can modify it, or ask you to go further, or ask you to take it in a new direction. But do not, do not, do not, give him a nothing little waddle. Because then, you know what you will be? You will be out of a job."

He returned to his stool and held up his hands. "Okay, again. Same physical states, but deliver them. Deliver them up for your audience."

After class I went up to Morales. "I don't know anything about pregnancy," I told him. "I mean, I know the basics, but I don't know how it feels or what people go through. So I was wondering—"

"Yes?" He looked at me but his eyes were hard.

"I was wondering how you're supposed to get to that point where you can deliver, like you said. How you get some place when you've never been there."

"What you do is you fake it," he answered. "And then as soon as you're out of rehearsal, you run to the bookstore. And you read. And you talk to pregnant women. And you make sure you know every detail there is to know about pregnancy before it's time to go to work again. Because one day of weakness is understandable. But a second—that's just irresponsible."

"Isn't there a craft involved?" I asked. "A way of doing it that you can teach us?"

Morales shouldered his bag. "I *am* teaching it to you. It seems to me you are making it more difficult than it has to be."

"But how did you learn to do what you do?" I wanted to know. "I mean, the shifting actors on stage, seeing how to make scenes better—how did you learn it?"

He looked at his watch. "I'm a busy person," Morales said. "Just come to class and listen, all right? I know you're enthusiastic, but this isn't a private tutorial."

EVER SINCE Reanne's scolding, I behaved myself in *Midsummer* rehearsals: I was off-book early, communed seriously with the forest spirits whenever I was on tree duty, and developed a macho walk and a nasal tone of voice for Peter Quince. I even tried to explain to the lamentable girl playing Titania that her character was in love with the donkey because of its prodigious male equipment. But it was all in vain. *Midsummer* established itself fully and probably permanently as a denizen of Suckville. A perfect sequel to *Bedsheet Oedipus*.

But here is something important to understand about Wildewood: even when I was feeling indignant, humiliated, talentless, dismayed about unitards, whatever—I wasn't miserable. Far from it. I was *alive* there, not stuck in the razzle-dazzle–deprived silence of Ohio. Conversations mattered at Wildewood, people felt strongly, and the moments of despair or embarrassment were followed, always, by times of palpable excitement.

There was the day Nanette and I went to a gospel concert for evening rec—one of the few nights she wasn't in *Show Boat* rehearsal, and we loved that big Jesus-y sound so much we stood up on our red velvet chairs, clapping and dancing and waving our hands in the air as the choir sang "When the Saints Go Marching In." When we turned around (we were near the front) we saw that the whole audience was on their seats behind us, and we all sang with the choir on "Loves Me Like a Rock."

Or when Iz and I went to dinner several nights in full Restoration Squash-your-boobs-up regalia—white powdered wigs, corsets, fake beauty marks, and all. Or when Jade and I grabbed brooms from a supply closet and reenacted the "Bushel and a Peck" dance, impromptu in the hall, while Demi and Lyle harmonized the song, Demi in full falsetto.

Or when I dared Candie, Iz, and Nanette to sing "Supercalifragilisticexpialidocious" at top volume in the hallways at seven in the morning, banging on everyone's doors, and they did it, and I had to buy them each a chocolate bar every day for five days. Or when we lay on the grass by the path, speaking in French accents to the boys who walked by.

Or this: one day, I took a bathroom break during Singing. Walking down the hall of the rehearsal building, I passed three other classes. Piano music thumped through the closed doors, and as I got closer I heard one group doing scales, one stumbling through harmonies to "What a Piece of Work Is Man," and the other in gleeful chorus, soaring through the syncopations of "One" from *A Chorus Line*. Inside the next room, which had an open door, Tamar and her assistant were marking out steps for *Cats*, which would rehearse there in the afternoon. Just before the bathroom, the hall was clogged with a rack of *Show Boat* costumes: frilly gowns with huge skirts, brown sackcloth jackets, and a row of pink parasols hanging by their handles. I stopped and fingered the polyester sleeve of one of the dresses, touched the rhinestones on their necklines, listened to the rustle of fabrics, barely audible over the "Five, six, seven, eight" coming from the choreographer's practice and the music from the classrooms. Even an ordinary hallway in need of a paint job was alive with glitter and sweat. Every single day at Wildewood was music, dance, comedy, *drama*.

So despite what happened later, remember this: I never, ever wanted to go home.

(click, shuffle, bang)

Sadye: Demi! Don't drop it.

Demi: Darling, I already dropped it.

Sadye: You lose your microcassette privileges. I'm holding it.

Demi: Okay, but I'm in the middle. We'll get better sound if I hold it.

Sadye: Okay, take it. But don't drop it again.

(shuffle, muffle)

Demi: It's July eighteenth, we think, and we're documenting the late-night stargazing ritual. Sadye, Lyle, Theo, Nanette, and I are currently on the roof of the boys' dorm--

Lyle: As we are most nights--

Demi: --until Farrell comes up and kicks the girls out.

Theo: Well, Theo is new.

Sadye: It's only his second night.

Lyle: We're corrupting him. We

expect it to be an easy task, however.

Nanette: Pounce!

Sadye: Shut up, Nanette!

Theo: What?

Nanette: Never mind. Theo, tell me something. Are you going with Bec?

Theo: What?

Lyle: Ooh, I didn't know he might be attached when I invited him up here. Am I out of the loop?

Theo: No.

Nanette: I've seen you with her a lot, that's all. I like to know things about people I share this roof with. And now that it looks like you're going to be a regular, I need to find out your status. Will you be bringing your girl up?

Sadye: Nanette!

Theo: She's not my girl. We--um. We've hung around together a couple times. She's got a boyfriend back home.

Demi: If you're having trouble with the ladies, Theo--Lyle and

I have some advice for you.

Lyle: *(giggling)*

Theo: What?

Demi: You need to wear some tighter pants.

Theo: Ha!

Demi: I'm serious! You have got to show your shape more.

Sadye: Ignore them, darling. They just want to see your buns for their own gay purposes.

Nanette: Okay, Theo. One more question. What's your favorite kind of ice cream?

Sadye: Nanette!

Theo: Um--

Demi: I love all ice cream. I am an equal opportunity ice-cream lover.

Lyle: An ice-cream slut, that's what you are.

Demi: It's true. Peanut butter, coconut, rum raisin--even the nasty flavors, I still like them.

Lyle: I have a favorite flavor.

Demi: You do?

Lyle: Chocolate. Like you, baby.

Demi: Aw, that's so sweet. Isn't he sweet?

Nanette: Lover boys, I was asking Theo. Not you.

Sadye: Yeah, I want to hear what Theo says, actually.

Theo: I'm gonna go with mint chocolate chip.

Nanette: Ooh! I knew it!

Sadye: Shut up!

Demi: Oh, I get it now! He likes mint chocolate chip!

Sadye: Sorry, Theo. They're being ridiculous. Do you want a beer?

Theo: Yeah, actually. Sure.

Demi: Me too.

Lyle: Me three.

(the sound of clinking bottles)

Theo: I've been meaning to ask you guys. Does Farrell turn a blind eye to the beer, or what?

Lyle: Exactly. A blind eye.

Theo: Do you pay him off?

Demi: *(shocked)* No!

Lyle: Ooh, maybe we should.

Demi: So far, he's been cool.

Lyle: We could pay him off in beer.

Demi: He hasn't seen the beer,
Theo. Lyle is teasing you.

Lyle: It's true. We hide the beer.
But I doubt he'd do anything if
he saw it.

Sadye: Where's Iz? For documentation
purposes, Iz and Candie are
sometimes here as well.

Nanette: Iz was taking a shower
and going to bed.

Demi: Morales is working her
crazy hard in *Birdie*. She
showed the "Spanish Rose"
number tonight and he's got
her dancing on the tables and
doing counterpoint rhythms
with those little clickety--
what are they?

Sadye: Castanets.

Demi: Castanets. Yeah. It's gonna
be good.

Nanette: Candie's not even out of
rehearsal yet. *Little Shop* is
having technical problems with
the man-eating plant.

Sadye: Back to documenting.

Lyle: Do we have to document?

Sadye: It's for posterity.

Theo: Why are you documenting? I mean it's cool, obviously, but why?

Demi: We're all gonna be famous some day.

Sadye: Well, speak for yourself.

Demi: We are, all of us. Isn't it obvious?

Sadye: I'm just saying, the odds are against every single one of us being famous.

Demi: Not true. Look at John Cusack and Jeremy Piven and Joan Cusack. They all went to drama school together.

Theo: They did?

Demi: Absolute fact. And Steve Pink, too, who wrote *High Fidelity* and *Grosse Pointe Blank*.

Lyle: I never heard of Steve Pink.

Demi: That's because you're an ignoramus.

Lyle: You call me an ignoramus because you're jealous of my superior theater history knowledge.

Demi: If you haven't heard of Steve Pink, you're at least a little bit of an ignoramus.

Lyle: That's it. I'm going to the computer lab and Googling him tomorrow. I don't think Steve Pink even exists. I think you made him up.

Demi: I did not!

Sadye: Okay, enough, you two. Everyone lie down on your backs and I'm going to make you serenade me in harmony.

Nanette: Excellent. What are we singing this time?

Sadye: "The Telephone Hour." Does everyone know it?

Theo: Of course.

Nanette: Of course.

Lyle: Of course. Anyone who doesn't know "The Telephone Hour" is an ignoramus.

(shuffle, click)

On JULY 27TH, Nanette was scheduled to head off to her *Secret Garden* audition in Los Angeles. She got permission to miss a day in order to do it, and her father Fed-Ex'd her sheet music because she had to learn a new audition piece to show she could sing the difficult music in the play. She rehearsed a song from *Into the Woods* with the M-TAP teacher. She was taking an early morning cab to the airport, flying to California, and doing the audition that same afternoon.

The day before she was meant to go, I came into the dorm after dinner to find her sitting on her bottom bunk and holding my tape recorder.

"What's up?" I said, pulling off my sneakers.

"I listened to the tape," she answered.

"Were we so ridiculous?" I said. "I can't believe you asked Theo about the ice cream!"

"I mean, I heard what you and Bec and those guys were saying about me. At the costume fitting for *Guys and Dolls.*"

Damn.

I knew I'd been snarky and jealous. We all had.

What kind of idiot was I to record all that and save it?

"I'm sorry," I said. "We were being evil."

"But we had that talk," Nanette sniffed. "I thought you were on my side."

"I am." I sat down on the bunk, guilt washing over me. "That was before."

"They said they wanted to poison my lemonade. Dawn wanted to *shoot* me."

"I didn't say that!"

"No, but you sat there while they did. And you said, what was it, why did I have to even come here already? And maybe I'd get sick and go home."

It was true. "I was sick jealous, Nanette," I told her. "Those were horrible things to say."

"That's right, they were."

"I'm sorry. You—you have no idea how it feels to be anything but the star."

"That's not true!" she cried. "I wasn't the star of *Night Music*. I wasn't the star of *Fiddler*."

"But those were national productions," I said. "You were like, the only kid."

"I wasn't the star of *Annie* most of the time, either. I told you I knew how it felt. That night when we talked about it."

"Nanette, look. I'm not saying we didn't do something wrong, something mean, but we—"

"I thought we were friends."

"We are. I never should have said that stuff."

"So why did you?"

"I—I've been having a hard time here. It's like everyone's better than I am at everything, and you're the best of anyone."

"No, I'm not."

"Yes, you are," I said. "And don't pretend you don't know it."

Nanette tossed the cassette recorder at me. "You should have stood up for me. Even Iz was nicer than you, and Adelaide was the part she wanted."

It was the part I had wanted, too. Nanette just didn't remember.

"A real friend would be happy for someone else's success."

"I'm sorry," I said again. "I really am."

"Sorry's not good enough," said Nanette.

She ran out of the room and slammed the door.

SHE DIDN'T come in until after curfew that night, and left for California early the next morning. I had no idea how to make it up to her, and Iz didn't either.

At seven thirty that evening, though, I was in our dorm room after dinner, and the hall phone rang.

"Candie Berkolee!" someone yelled in the hallway. "Candie Berkolee! Telephone."

"She's not here," I said, sticking my head out the doorway. "She's a principal." Meaning she had night rehearsal.

The girl on the phone said something into it. "Isadora Feingold!" she yelled. "Is Isadora around? Phone call."

"She's not here, either."

The girl listened to the telephone and looked at me. "It's your roommate Nanette," she said after a minute. "She needs to talk to someone."

"She doesn't want to talk to me," I said, "I don't think."

"No, she doesn't," said the girl. "But you should take it anyway. Something's going on."

I took the phone. Nanette was crying.

"I lost my wallet," she sobbed. "I thought it was in my bag, but now I don't have it. I don't have any ID."

"Where are you?" I asked.

"LAX," she sniffed. "A cab dropped me off here, and I ate a slice of pizza in the food court, and then when I went to go buy magazines I didn't have my wallet anymore. I went to lost and found and everything."

"Oh, no."

"They won't let me on the plane without ID. And now I've missed the plane, I was looking for it for so long. I looked all over the food court, and the newsstand, and on the sidewalk outside. The people at lost and found were totally unhelpful."

"Isn't someone with you? Doesn't the theater like, shepherd you around?"

"No. I got a cab on my own."

"What do they say at the airplane desk?"

"I have to show ID. They'll let me on the next plane with my old ticket, but not unless I have my driver's license."

"Do you have any money?"

"No."

"A bank card?"

"No. My dad is going to kill me."

"You have to call him."

"I'm scared."

"Nanette, you have to. Maybe he can vouch for your identification or fax your passport," I said.

"He's going to be so mad." She was still crying. "I—last year, when I was on tour, I did the same thing. Lost my wallet with all my ID and cards and cash, and he was like, so pissed off at how disorganized I am."

"Listen. There's no way you can get home if you don't call him," I said. "I'm going to wait here by the phone."

"I don't know."

"He would never want you stuck in the L.A. airport all alone. That's what your cell phone is for, right? For emergencies. He wants you to call him. Trust me."

Nanette started crying again. "It's that . . ." She choked and had trouble getting the words out. "He, he, he wants me to be *professional.* I can just hear him." She lowered her voice. "'Do you think Sarah Jessica Parker lost her wallet when she was in *Annie?* Do you think Daisy Eagan spaced out on the way home from her *Secret Garden* audition? No, of course they didn't. People who space out like that don't get jobs. And if they get them, they don't keep them.'"

"Nanette—"

"You don't understand, Sadye. Your parents actually like you. Mine don't even know me. They didn't even drive out to see *Guys and Dolls*, because my brother had a film audition and my sister booked a commercial."

"Ugh."

"I haven't lived with them in a year. Kylie even has my room."

"Oh."

"Yeah. When I was there for a week before coming here, I slept on the foldout."

"Ouch."

"I'm like a work pony to them. 'Send Nanette on the road, and she'll send her paycheck home.' That's what it's about. The only reason they sent me to Wildewood is because *Fiddler* ended and I didn't get the last three jobs I was up for. They figured this way, at least, I'd get seen by Morales, 'cause he's gonna direct the Lemony Snicket musical next spring and they want me to go for that."

"Well, you know he likes you," I said. "So it's probably worth it."

"I'm just all by myself in this," Nanette said. "Like I'm not even a kid anymore. Like I have to be this perfect grown-up all the time, and I'm always moving around. And if I don't get *Secret Garden*, I don't even know what I'll do with myself. It'll be like four strikes in their eyes, and they're not going to be pleased."

"Look," I told her. "Calling your dad is the only thing to do. You're gonna be okay. I'm going to sit here, and I want you to call me back."

We hung up. I sunk down on the floor of the hall, waiting.

Eventually the phone rang again, and I answered it. "Okay, I did it," said Nanette. "He's faxing my passport. But he is so mad, Sadye, you have no idea."

"What time does your new plane get in?"

"Four a.m. into Rochester," she said. "But I don't know how I'm gonna get back to Wildewood from the airport."

"Don't worry about that," I promised. "I'll make sure someone's there to meet you."

* * *

I MARCHED over to the administration offices to talk to the summer institute secretary, so he could arrange a car for Nanette—but it was after eight o'clock; no one was there. So I went to the *Midsummer* rehearsal room and walked in without knocking. The guy who played Puck was crouching in a feral, feline position, delivering a monologue, while Theo (Lysander) and Rosa (Helena) sat with their backs to the wall, looking bored and waiting to rehearse their scenes.

Reanne held up a hand, signing that I should not interrupt until Puck had finished, and I did wait a couple of minutes, but when he got to the end and she leaned forward and began talking to him about his movement vocabulary, I couldn't stand it. Weepy Nanette was taking a six-hour plane flight all alone at night and then had no way to get back to Wildewood, and these people were babbling at each other about whether Puck would put his hand on his knees or if that was too baseballish. I tapped Reanne on the shoulder.

She breathed a long sigh and asked Puck to hold it. "What do you want?"

I explained the situation, saying how they had to take responsibility for Nanette.

"Okay," said Reanne. "You tried the administration offices?"

"They're all shut up."

"All right. Let me make a phone call."

Reanne told the cast they could take a break, and called someone—maybe Morales—from her cell.

"It wasn't that the audition ran late," she said. "The girl lost her wallet."

Reanne turned to me to check that she had her story straight. I nodded, adding, "You need to send a car for her."

"The whole campus is going to be asleep when she gets back," Reanne said into the phone. "Someone's going to have to stay up to let her in the dorms."

The person on the other line said something, and Reanne chuckled. "So long as it's not me."

I interrupted again. "The point is, Nanette can't pay for a cab. She'll be stuck if you don't send a car for her."

"Shh." Reanne waved at me, trying to get me to shut up.

"She's gonna be so exhausted; she's getting in at like, the middle of the night." I thrust a piece of paper forward, on which I'd written Nanette's new flight number and its arrival time. "And she only flew out this morning. She needs someone to go get her."

"Hold on," Reanne said into the phone. "Sadye, I know you're concerned for your friend, but you must see that she made a real mess of what should have been a simple trip."

"So?"

"So we're discussing who should take responsibility, and what the possibilities are."

"I don't see why you're not calling a car service now and getting it taken care of!" I yelled. "It's not like she doesn't know she messed up. She knows! She feels like an idiot! She needs a ride home!"

"I'll ring you back in a few," Reanne muttered, clicking off her cell.

"You have to order her a car," I said, more softly. "She has no way to get here otherwise."

Reanne crossed her arms and looked at me. "There is plenty of time, Sadye. Her plane hasn't even taken off and it's a six-hour flight."

"But why won't you order it?" I asked. "I want to call her back before she gets on the plane, so she knows it'll be there."

"It wouldn't hurt you to say 'Please,' Sadye," Reanne finally muttered. "It wouldn't hurt you to say 'Hey, Reanne, I'm sorry to interrupt your rehearsal.'"

I looked at Reanne. She was kind, and a bit silly; willing to leap around the woods making woo woo noises and pretending to be a fairy. She was never harsh or bossy with the actors—and she was sweetly encouraging to the lowliest trees at all times. She had dealt with my insurrection, my interruptions, my criticisms—usually with patience and flattery, and never with more than mild annoyance.

I liked her.

I thought she was a bad director.

I began to cry. "I know I'm being dramatic," I sobbed. "But I owe Nanette, okay? I did something awful to her; I was jealous of her all summer, jealous of how she sings, and how she looks, and her talent, and all the chances she's had. I've been jealous of Lyle for having Demi, and of Demi for having Lyle, and of Iz and Candie for their voices, and jealous of everyone's parts and—"

Reanne put her arm around me and led me to a folding chair.

"It's just that I'm nobody here," I went on. "I could disappear. I could leave tomorrow. It wouldn't even matter to anyone. I loved *Guys and Dolls*, I loved it, but I could have left the show and nobody would have noticed."

"That's not true," Reanne said sympathetically. "You're a very important part of our community."

"Morales doesn't even know my name. Every single one of my friends has a lead. I'm surrounded by the most talented people here, and there's nothing I can do to make a difference," I sobbed. "I try to talk to you about *Midsummer*, I try over and over to share ideas in rehearsal, or in acting class—and no one wants to hear what I say. There's no difference I can make anywhere at Wildewood—except this."

"Come, come."

"I just want to help my friend," I said. "It's like the only thing I can do."

"Take a deep breath," said Reanne. "I promise you we'll get Nanette home."

"I want to be irreplaceable," I said, sniffing. "I want to be a person that matters."

"Actors are never irreplaceable, Sadye," said Reanne. "It's in the nature of the job: they have to be replaced. Shows are recast all the time. They run for months, people get other jobs, new actors step in. If you need to be irreplaceable, you shouldn't be an actor."

NANETTE got back safely. She tiptoed into our dorm at nearly dawn. Before she got into bed, she put a stack of Hershey's Kisses on my pillow. They were freebies in the backseat of the Town Car Wildewood sent for her.

* * *

TWO DAYS LATER, something awful and wonderful happened. A girl named Amy had to be sent home. She wasn't eating enough, and she was working too hard, given what she was eating, and one day she couldn't get out of bed, she was so tired and worn down. Her room-mates said she had a headache the first day but soon it became apparent that she was on the verge of anorexia and starting to lose it, and had to go back to Connecticut for a bit of rest and psychotherapy.

The next morning, as I sat on the floor stretching before dance class, Tamar came and asked me if I wanted Amy's part: Rumpleteazer.

Rumpleteazer is one of a comical pair of raucous cats (the other is Mungojerrie) who dance a ridiculous dance while someone else sings how they are knock-about clowns so clever they steal meat from their own family's oven.

"You'll have to learn it nights," Tamar said, "and skip the evening recreation quite a few days; then we'll have to juggle the dress rehearsal schedules to make sure you can be in both *Cats* and *Midsummer*, but we've done it before, other years, and we're sure it can be managed. Though it's rather a lot to take on. What do you say, Sadye?"

It crossed my mind that Reanne had told Tamar

how unhappy I was. They could have easily filled this role with someone already in the cast; there was no need to give it to me.

But I didn't care if it was charity. I'd take it.

I got to skip *Midsummer* rehearsal that afternoon to learn the basics of the Rumpleteazer part. It was the best afternoon I'd had at Wildewood. Jade from Hot Box Girls was playing Mungojerrie. She was quite small, and Amy had been, too. Tamar started reworking her choreography on the spot to take advantage of the new difference in our heights. Jade jumped up to stand on my knee, rode on me piggyback, ran through my legs. It was so fascinating to see Tamar working on the fly like that, and to know that she was making use of who I was—customizing the dance to suit me.

Jade and I went to dinner sweaty and happy. We were starving and ate big plates of lame institutional spaghetti like it was the best meal we'd ever tasted.

This is what it's supposed to be like, I thought. This is what I came here for.

Sadye: It's July twenty-ninth.
Demi, Nanette, Sadye, and Lyle
on the roof again.
Lyle: It's a beautiful starry
night. The moon is out.

Nanette: And look at us. Sadye and I are here with two gorgeous and completely ineligible boys.

Demi: Hey, what happened to that Theo boy you like? The one who hides his buns? He came up twice. But now he's--

Nanette: Yeah, where is he these days?

Demi: He's in absentia!

Sadye: Publicize it, why don't you?

Demi: We all know you like him.

Sadye: That was just an early crush. I only like him as a friend now.

Lyle: Hardly.

Sadye: What? How do you know?

Lyle: You give him the puppy-dog eye in *Midsummer* all the time when you're being a tree. You're like a tree puppy dog.

(Sadye pinches Lyle)

Lyle: Ow!

Sadye: I am not a tree puppy dog! I am a master of subtleness and concealing my emotions.

Nanette: Ahem.

Sadye: What?

Nanette: Not.

Sadye: Okay, I still like him.

Lyle: Okay, you're not really a puppy dog. Demi told me you like him.

Sadye: Demi!

Demi: He made me tell!

Lyle: I forced the details out of him. I have unspeakable methods of torture.

Demi: It's true. He's a bad, bad man.

Lyle: Look, I'll demonstrate. Stand back, my friends, for a public exhibition of tried-and-true methods for getting Demi Howard to tell you all his friends' secrets.

(Lyle pinches Demi.)

Demi: Ow! You know you're not allowed to pinch me there! That's cheating!

Nanette: Where did he pinch you?

Demi: You don't want to know.

Lyle: On the leg, just above the knee.

Nanette: No one ever pinches me.

Demi: I'll pinch you.

Nanette: I don't want you.

Demi: Why not?

Nanette: I want a hetero boy to pinch me.

Lyle: Want me to go downstairs and find you one? I can do it. I know for a fact that Frankie lives on the top floor. It would take me like forty seconds to get him to come up here and pinch you.

Nanette: No! No!

Lyle: Prime hetero pinching from Frankie. What more are you asking for? I can deliver it right away!

Sadye: We're degenerating, seriously.

Nanette: Do *not* go and ask Frankie to pinch me.

Lyle: Okay, okay. I was just trying to help.

Sadye: Nanette, you don't need pinching. I've got no pinching. Look at me!

Nanette: What?

Sadye: We don't need pinching. We can be happy without boys.

Nanette: Aw, come on. If Theo pinched you, you wouldn't be anti-pinch. You be totally pro-pinch.

Sadye: Well, that's Theo. That's not generalized pinching. That's Theo pinching.

Nanette: What's the difference?

Sadye: The difference is you're not supposed to want general love. You're supposed to want love from someone in particular.

Nanette: Is that feminism?

Sadye: Maybe. I don't know. Isn't it just self-confidence? Like, you don't need a man.

Lyle: What, Sadye, don't you need us? We need you!

Demi: Since when is pinching the same as love? Pinching is not the same as love.

Sadye: It is in *this* conversation.

Nanette: I don't care if I'm *supposed* to want it or not want it. I just want it. Love from hetero boys, love from

audience members, love from
the world.

Lyle: But not from Frankie.

Nanette: That's right.

Sadye: We love you, Nanette. Isn't
that enough?

Nanette: No. I want hetero boys
and the whole world.

Sadye: I better turn this recorder
off before we say anything more
incriminating.

(shuffle, click)

ℕANETTE could cry on cue. "I taught myself after I made this straight-to-video movie," she told us at lunch one day.

"Wait, you were in a movie?" Demi asked

"Oh, yeah, but it was a little part and it sucked," said Nanette. "It's my sister who's going to have the movie career, probably. At least that's what my dad says." She drank some cranberry juice and went on. "Anyway, the director was this complete jerk, and this boy and I had a scene where we had to cry because our mom was dead—it was like a mystery thriller—"

"Who else was in it?" Demi wanted to know.

"Oh, that guy from TV, Michael Rapaport; it doesn't matter, I didn't get to meet him," said Nanette. "I was just in the one scene. Anyway, we had to cry and whatever, I was like twelve and the kid was only six, and I guess this director didn't work with kids a lot, because we weren't crying, and we weren't crying—I mean, we tried, but we couldn't—and the boy started laughing, and the director just yelled and screamed at us, telling us we were awful actors and bad people and he was disgusted by us—until we both started to cry for real. Then he rolled the cameras, got the shots he needed, and told us we'd done a great job."

"That's horrible."

"Whatever. It happens all the time on films." said Nanette. "Because they need the shot, and you're wasting everyone's money if you can't do it. So then I spent like a million hours looking in the bathroom mirror and learning how to make myself cry on cue. So now if they ask me to cry, I say, 'Which eye do you want?'"

"How do you do it?" asked Demi.

"I used to think about how my brother died—I had this brother who died when I was like four and he was six—but now I just think *Cry*—and I do."

"Do it," said Demi.

"Yes, do it!" I pushed.

And Nanette did. She wiped her mouth delicately,

stared into space, and then her face crumpled and tears started dripping down her cheeks.

Then we felt bad. Or at least I did. I mean, Nanette has spent most of her life being a trick pony for grown-ups. She didn't need to be a trick pony for her only friends.

STILL, when Morales announced in class that we were going to spend a few days working toward crying on cue, I was interested. I thought, if I can do this, then I'll know I'm an actress—and none of the badness of this acting class will matter.

If I can do this, I'll know I belong here.

"There are four approaches to crying for the actor," Morales announced, striding back and forth in front of us as we sat on the floor. "One. You call up a miserable life experience in your past. You imagine it, focus on it, until you feel like crying. This might be useful for film actors who have to do a reaction shot, but it'll take you out of the moment when you're playing a part onstage, because when you're onstage you need to stay in character. That's why I don't believe in the Method, and why I don't teach it.

"Two. A variation on the first one. You imagine

your mother dead, your dog dead, your best friend. Not something that happened, but something hypothetical. You do it with intense concentration until you cry. I have problems with teaching this approach, as I have problems with the Method approach, because it takes you out of character. But you can see that it involves some imaginative projection, rather than dredging up memories, so it is closer to acting, as I see it.

"Three. You learn what crying looks like. The lower lip quivers. The crier clamps the lips together as if trying to stop. He looks down. Blinks back the tears. You take some time to look at yourself crying and you note the expression so minutely that you can mimic it on demand. Very often tears will follow once the rest of your body is there.

"Four. You enter so deeply into a character's inner life that you weep because your character weeps. You feel the emotions of your character and cry because he needs to cry.

"So: I posit that if we begin with the second approach—and you cry, then we can take a moment and study ourselves in this state. We can master the particular physiognomy of our own tears—what do the shoulders do? What do the facial muscles do? Where do the hands want to go? And begin to replicate them, as one does in approach number three. Practicing this imaginative projection and then self-observation will make you more fluid, more open to the emotions you'll need for a character who's going to cry. Then we'll take that fluidity and we'll work on new monologues for the rest of the summer, so you guys can get to the point of approach number four, where your character's emotions can take you to that point. Got it? Good."

He dimmed the lights and had us all lie on the floor. Then he took us on a guided visualization—like those Reanne had done at the start of *Midsummer* rehearsals—only this one was designed to make us weep. We were at war, he said. Our homes were vandalized by enemy soldiers. We were to picture our own homes, our own parents, our living rooms.

And then our furniture trashed, our belongings set fire.

Our parents murdered. Our bodies violated.

Our dogs and cats strung up by the neck.

Within ten minutes I was crying, half from the visualization, and half from a mad and frustrated urge to run out of the rehearsal room. It felt so wrong being trapped in there and forced to imagine these horrible catastrophes. I longed to stand up, yank open the door, and walk out of Morales's classroom forever. Just to go into the sunlight and the air, away from this fabricated horror.

"You may sit up now," said Morales. "I'm going to raise the lights a bit, and I want you to move over to the mirrors and find a space for yourself. Look at your face. Look at your backs, your legs, your shoulders, your hands. Feel the rhythms of your breath, remember how your throat feels. Sense memory, people, sense memory."

I got up and walked to the mirror, tears still streaming down my face. I could see that some people were crying and others were not, but I didn't feel the sense of accomplishment I'd thought I'd feel if I managed to cry.

I felt manipulated and angry. Trapped.

Because I had to stay. If I walked out now, how could I come back? It would be like walking out on my dream of being onstage. Admitting failure just when I'd finally had a glimpse of what it felt like to be part of a decent show.

And yet, I hated what Morales had made us do. It wasn't anything I'd ever wanted, to have my emotions jerked around like that by someone I didn't even like. It wasn't what I'd meant when I'd asked him how to get there.

I sat, crying and staring at myself in the mirror.

Finally he brought up the lights and asked us to discuss the physical qualities we'd noticed in ourselves, whether we'd actually wept or not. People raised their hands and said stuff. I wasn't listening.

As we filed out of class, Morales tapped me on the shoulder. I stayed while everyone else went out. "You made progress today," he said. "You should be proud of yourself."

For a second I thought, Oh, thank goodness he's noticed me. He thinks I'm improving. Tamar must have told him I'm good as Rumpleteazer. I'm improving, I'm an actress; Mr. Jacob Morales thinks well of me.

And then I remembered how I felt, and I said, almost without meaning to: "I had a problem with the exercise, actually."

"What?"

"Your actors might trust you to direct a play, because you're very good at what you do—"

"Of course they do," he said.

"I admired you so much when this all started," I said. "A real Broadway director, someone who can make a show click. But now—maybe this exercise works when a group of students has terrific trust in a teacher, maybe it works when people aren't afraid to walk out if they can't stand it, but you—we're terrified of you."

"Pardon me?"

"All I could think about while I was lying there was that it gave you some kind of joy to make all of us cry."

"What?"

"You were manipulating us, like puppets. And none of us had the guts to leave, because you control our lives here."

"You can't deny it had an effect on you."

"Maybe it did—but you can't take a whole group of kids who are scared sick of you and then make them feel like their parents are dead and their pets are strung up by the neck. It's not right. It's not acting."

Morales held up his hand to stop me. "That's enough. This is not your place." He walked to the door. "Your place here is to study and learn. I'm sorry to see you're so blocked and so angry, Sadye, but it's none of my concern."

And he was gone.

Thing was, part of me felt happy that he knew my name.

I WANTED to talk to Demi about what happened. I ran out to look for him, but he'd already gone to his singing class, which was different from mine.

I went through the rest of the day with this strange adrenaline rush from my argument with Morales. Went to lunch with Nanette and Candie, *Midsummer* rehearsal, Restoration Comedy, dinner with the girls from that class, and an hour of *Cats* rehearsal, eight to nine p.m.

They let me and Jade out to make room for another group of dancers, and we went back to the dorms. None of my friends would be back from rehearsal for an hour or more. I took a shower and changed into regular clothes.

Then I went outside with the intention of going up to the boys' roof with a flashlight and a book until everyone else got free.

Before I reached the stairs, though, I ran into Theo.

"Hey," he said. "I thought you were at *Cats*."

"Got out early."

Theo smiled. "I heard you talked back to Morales."

I nodded. I had told Nanette at lunch, and Nanette could never keep her mouth shut. I changed the subject. "Didn't you have *Midsummer* principals?"

"Reanne let us out." He shrugged. "She wants to work Bottom and Titania. That girl still has no idea what she's talking about."

"Titania?"

"Yeah. I wish someone would explain to her what her speeches mean."

"I tried."

"Really?"

"I think I was nice about it. But she was un-amused."

"That's our Sadye."

"What?"

"Poking in the nose."

"What, am I obnoxious?"

"Maybe."

"I am?"

"A little."

"You think I'm obnoxious?"

"That came out wrong."

"What right way is there to tell someone she's obnoxious?" I asked, hurt.

"I didn't say obnoxious. You said obnoxious," answered Theo. "I mean . . ." He sighed. "Here. Come walk with me. Don't be mad, you're not obnoxious." He took my arm and walked us out of the dorm and down the path toward the dance studios. "You care, right?" he said. "You speak up. That's why you complained to Morales about that acting exercise, that's why you kvetch at Reanne, that's why you try and help Titania. All this stuff matters to you. I don't see anyone else caring that much."

"Reanne thinks I need to be more of an ensemble player," I said. "She said maybe I shouldn't be an actor if I need to be irreplaceable."

"Nah," Theo said as we walked into the open dance studio where we'd first met. "You have strong opinions. That can be good in a lot of contexts."

"But not in this one."

"I don't know." Theo sat down at the baby grand and played a few chords. "What do you want to hear?"

"How about 'Seasons of Love'?"

"Ah, *Rent*. Yes, I can play *Rent*," he answered. And launched into it.

I sat on the piano bench next to him, watching his fingers move across the keys. Wondering what they'd feel like if he ever touched me. Listening to this music about time passing, looking at all the ways we measure our lives—in minutes or moments of connection, cups of coffee, bridges burned. In love.

I didn't want the summer to end. Even after what happened with Morales.

After "Seasons of Love," Theo played the intro to "Sue Me" from *Guys and Dolls*. "Sing," he told me.

I shook my head.

"Why not?"

"Because. If there's anything I've learned in my time here, it's that when people ask me if I sing, my answer should be no."

"Aw, I'm not asking if you sing," Theo said, vamping on the piano.

"Yes, you are."

"No." He took his fingers off the keys. "I'm asking you *to* sing."

"Oh."

"You know you love it. You should see the look on your face when music starts."

"I go flat," I told him. "And I don't have a lot of range. I was told to lip-synch the Hot Box numbers." I had never confessed that to anyone before. Not even to Demi.

"So?" Theo seemed unconcerned.

"So, I'm not a singer."

"This isn't an audition. This is you and me and the piano."

I remembered how before I got to Wildewood, Demi and I used to burst into song with zero encouragement. We'd sing on the bus, in the drugstore, walking down the street in Cleveland, jumping on his couch. I'd sing in the shower or while washing dishes. We'd sing along with movies on the DVD player. But here I had stopped. Of course I had to sing every other day in class, but that was always in a group. We did vocal exercises and learned harmonies. We never had to sing alone.

And anywhere but Singing, I had been silent. Making other people serenade me, directing them, dancing while they harmonized. Because I didn't want people to hear. All those people who could really sing.

Maybe my problem wasn't what Morales and Reanne implied—that I lacked humility. Maybe my problem was that I lacked confidence.

"Sadye, I'm vamping here." Theo was playing the introduction to "Sue Me" again, waiting for my Miss Adelaide to swing in with her list of lovelorn complaints.

Not that confidence would make me a singer when I didn't have the voice. It wouldn't. I would never have the voice.

Theo started singing the Adelaide part himself in a comical squalk. "Okay, okay," I said, shaking myself out of contemplation. "If you're that desperate to sing a duet, I suppose I can oblige you."

"I'm desperate!" he yelled. "My kingdom for a duet!"

"Shut up!"

He started over with the vamp. "No, you. Shut up and sing."

And so I sang.

And Theo sang.

We sang together, easily, 'cause we'd heard the song a thousand times during rehearsal.

Then we sang "Money, Money" from the movie of *Cabaret*, and "Anything You Can Do" from *Annie Get Your Gun*, though we messed up the lyrics.

It was so, so fun. I missed the high notes, and at first I was embarrassed, but then I didn't care.

When we finished "Anything You Can Do," I pretended to collapse on the floor from exhaustion. "It's nearly curfew," I said, pointing to the clock on the studio wall.

"Nearly, but not."

"Demi and those guys will be wondering where I am, up on the roof."

He shrugged.

"Do you wanna go?"

Theo shook his head. "Nah, I'll stay here. You go along."

What? Why wouldn't he want to come? After we'd just had such a good time. "I can't figure you out," I finally said.

"What? I'm an open book."

"No, you're not."

"What do you mean?"

I stood up and paced the room. "First you offer to come back to my dorm with me, then you won't even dance with me. Next you walk with me in the moonlight and then sprint off like I've got cooties.

Then you show up at the cast party with Bec."

"Sadye—"

"I'm not done," I said. "After that, you come up on the roof a couple times, tell everybody you're single, and for some unknown reason, never show up again. And now you tell me I'm obnoxious, then drag me out here in the middle of the night." I folded my arms. "I can't tell what you think of me, Theo," I said. "And I have to say, I'm tired of worrying about it. Like me, don't like me, but don't play around with me."

Theo stood up from the piano. "I wasn't playing around."

"Oh, no?"

"I wasn't."

"Well, it feels like it from my end. Why don't you want to come up to the roof?"

"Because I want to stay here."

"Why?"

"Sadye."

"What?"

"Sadye." He stood up. "I think you're—" He crossed the dance floor, reached out and grabbed my hand, pulled me in close, and breathed the words into my neck. "I think you're—whatever I think of to say sounds like a line. But—"

"But what?" I asked. Theo's hands were on my

shoulders. His lips were almost on my ear. Was he pouncing?

"You're funny, you're unusual," whispered Theo. "You're probably too smart for your own good."

"Oh."

"I think about you all the time."

"You have a lame way of showing it."

"What I want to know is—" Theo was still whispering. "There's something I've never had the guts to ask."

"What?"

He hesitated. "Are you taken?"

"Taken?" I stepped back in surprise. "By who?"

"By Demi."

"Demi's gay, Theo. He's with Lyle. Don't tell me you didn't know that. They're all over each other."

"You seem taken by him anyway."

"I do?"

"You put your arms around him. You dance with him. You talk about him like he's your boyfriend."

And I knew it was true.

It was true.

Part of me *was* taken by Demi, and maybe always would be. I loved him.

"I'm not taken by Demi," I whispered in Theo's ear. "I've been waiting for you."

We kissed, there in the studio, trembling and nervous, with light from the streetlamps outside spilling through the window into squares of white on the floor.

I RAN INTO the girls' dorms just under curfew and threw myself into bed two seconds before the hall monitor called "lights out."

But I couldn't sleep.

Iz, Candie, and Nanette gossiped for a few minutes in the dark. Candie had recently moved her affections from the split personality half-monster *Jekyll & Hyde* to the psychotic dentist from *Little Shop of Horrors*. He had kissed her for real (not just onstage) about a week before, and she was filled with new emotion over his attentions.

I didn't want to tell them about Theo, somehow. Well, I wanted to tell Nanette , but I didn't want to deal with Iz's competitive streak or Candie's overenthusiasm. So I stayed quiet as Candie rattled on about the dentist, and when they drifted off to sleep, I grabbed my microcassette recorder and snuck out to knock on Demi's window.

He opened it—not asleep yet—and the two of us ninja'd up to the roof, keeping silent until we got through the door and shut it behind us.

"Hey," I said.

"Hey, hey! My Sadye!" Demi walked over to the corner where we stored our snacks under a pile of ratty wool blankets. "You're in luck. Beverages are still—well, still a bit colder than warm!"

"Who made the beer run, you or Lyle?"

"Me," he answered, handing me a beer and rummaging under the blanket. "They needed extra time with 'The Telephone Hour,' so they let me go early. We waited for you, but— Ooh, look. There are potato products left. Did you know you'd be so lucky?"

"Ooh, they had the sticks?"

"Sticks and . . . ripple-y chips and salt and vinegar."

"Amazing." I grabbed a blanket and spread it on the tar surface of the roof.

We settled on the blanket, lying side by side. "I kissed Theo," I told Demi. "Or Theo kissed me."

"Finally."

"Yeah," I said. "Finally."

"Did you get to feel his buns?"

"Demi!"

"I'm just asking. They're like a total mystery."

"No."

"The buns of mystery. The mysterious buns of Wildewood."

"Stop it. It was romantic."

"OOOOOhhh."

"It was!"

"No really, that's good," Demi said. "I'm happy for you. He seems all right."

"I wasn't asking for your approval."

"Sorry, did I say the wrong thing?"

"No," I said. "It wasn't about buns, that's all."

"Okay, I take it back about the buns. Forget I ever mentioned buns."

Neither of us said much for a bit. I turned and looked at Demi's beautiful profile, his nearly bald head curving into his sharp cheekbones, round nose, and full lips. Suddenly I wanted to kiss him.

Which was bizarre and wrong.

And he'd be grossed out anyway, I knew.

Besides which, he had a boyfriend.

Besides which, we were friends. And I loved Lyle.

Besides which, I had Theo now. I mean, I had just been kissing Theo.

Besides which—

I sat up and tried to make the feeling go away by opening the bag of potato chips. "Did you guys redo 'Sincere'?" I asked, referring to the choreography on one of Demi's solos.

"This afternoon," he answered, sitting up as well. "It's better the new way. How's *Cats*?"

"Good," I said happily. "I think it's gonna be good."

"I hear you had a fight with Morales."

"What? Not a fight. Did Nanette say fight?"

Demi shook his head and laughed. "I didn't get it from Nanette. It was all over the rehearsal room. No one's got secrets."

"I did tell him off."

"What did you say?"

I explained: how Morales manipulated people's feelings. How it wasn't a trusting environment. How he controlled our lives, had too much power over us. And even though I knew Demi loved Morales, even though we'd argued about it before, I still expected him to take my side.

Because we'd been best friends when neither of us had anyone else. Because we'd saved each other.

But he didn't take my side.

I guess he couldn't.

He was so far in at Wildewood, and so rewarded for being so far in—everything was going his way, he was the king and the true believer, both—that he laid into me all of a sudden. "Sadye," he said, "can I just say? No offense, but your attitude is bad."

"What?"

"You know I'm not the only one who thinks it, either. Lyle says you're always disrupting *Midsummer*—"

"What? I thought he liked my ideas."

"He does, but you're not a team player, you're always trying to say what you think instead of committing to the ensemble. And I've seen you sulking around in Acting, pouting when you don't get something right away, and you seem to think the world should *come* to you, like you shouldn't have to work for it. That's the whole point of this place, Sadye. You're here to work. To be humble. Not to have attitude and be all defensive all the time."

"But—"

Demi wouldn't let me. "You haven't had a great deal here, I know," he said. "But did you ever think that you bring that on yourself? You do well in dance class, and you give it your all, and what happens? You get the Hot Box Girl, you get Rumpleteazer. But everywhere else, you rock the boat. You complain and you criticize the people who are supposed to be teaching us, who are dedicating their time to teach us. In acting, in rehearsals, in a lot of situations, you act like you think you know better than everyone else."

"You don't know what it's like," I spat back. "You have no idea how it is not to have your talent. Not to have red carpets stretching out for you wherever you choose to put your feet."

"Yes, I do!" he answered. "I take dance class, where

everyone's better than I am. I take Pantomime. I don't know what I'm doing in those classes at all! And yeah, Morales is tough, and he's mean sometimes. But you know what I do? I shut my trap and I listen. I figure he's tough because the business is tough, and he has something to teach us. I dance as hard as I can. I don't prance around criticizing."

"It's not the same for you," I said. "You're Conrad Birdie. You're Sky Masterson."

"You don't have to be so bitter, is all I'm saying. You're complaining all the time and ruining experiences for other people."

"I'm not complaining!" I said—although I knew that sometimes I had been. "I'm trying to have a conversation. I think we need to be critical of what's going on here, not just lie back and accept whatever happens. Because otherwise what kind of artists are we?"

"We are *student* artists, Sadye. We're here to learn, not to disrupt everyone's experience because we feel insecure."

"Is that what you think I'm doing?" I cried. I wanted to explain that I disrupted *Midsummer* because I wanted it to be better. Because I had concrete ideas for how to make it better. That I wasn't settling for mediocrity. And—

"Look," Demi said, before I had collected my

thoughts. "Maybe this isn't the best time to tell you this, but I don't know when else to do it."

"What?" My skin felt cold and the roof seemed suddenly quiet.

"I'm staying," said Demi. "Here at Wildewood. I'm not going home to Brenton."

"What do you mean?"

"I filled out an application form, and they accepted me for the school year. I'm going to spend my senior year here with Lyle."

"No."

"Sadye, I'm sorry. You know I love you, but—"

"When did you decide?"

"I knew I wanted to stay here the minute classes started. I think I asked for the application at the end of the first week."

"Without telling me?"

"I—"

"But how can you leave me like this?" I went on pitifully. "I can't go back to Brenton without you."

"I can't go back there *at all*," said Demi.

"What do you mean?"

"Think about it, Sadye. My dad can't stand to look me in the face, and my mom is hardly any better. I have to fake who I am every minute I'm at school, and come home to people who wish I was someone else."

I nodded.

"Here . . ." Demi walked to the edge of the roof and looked down at the campus. "Here is like the family I was meant to have. I can be who I am. Do you see?"

"And there's Lyle."

"Yes, Lyle. And acting classes. And music. And theater history. And just . . . this place. I am never going back to Brenton."

"Why didn't you tell me?" I asked.

"I only found out I was in a couple days ago. I guess—I guess I wasn't sure you'd be happy for me, and I didn't want to spoil it by getting you all upset. You've been so judgmental about everything."

"I have not!"

He looked at me. "So jealous, then."

"I don't want you to leave me!" I yelled.

The door to the roof opened. It was Farrell the hall counselor. "Why is there shouting up here?" he asked. "It's after curfew. This is unacceptable, and—hey, is that beer? Do you two have *beer* up here?"

Demi and I stared at him. Silent.

Farrell walked over and picked up the six-pack of empties. "I can't believe you two. Don't you have any respect for the rules of this place?"

Demi smiled his most ingratiating smile. "Hey,

Farrell, we didn't mean to raise our voices, we—"

"Don't 'Farrell' me," he snapped. "I've been letting it slide with you guys hanging out on the roof, and sneaking around at night, and I've even been lax when you broke curfew—but underage drinking is far beyond what I'm willing to tolerate."

We nodded dumbly.

"Who bought this beer? Who bought it?"

I looked at Demi's terrified face, and knew that if he got caught, there was a good chance he wouldn't be allowed to go to Wildewood for the school year. Like that guy Lyle knew who got expelled for having a bottle of whiskey in his locker.

If he got caught, he'd have come back to Ohio with me.

If I let him tell the truth, I'd get to keep him. We'd be together, Lyle would be far away, we could be together all of senior year.

"I bought it," I told Farrell.

"You did? Where?"

"The convenience store, down the way from the stone fence."

"The Cumberland Farms?"

"Yeah."

He squinted at me. "You're telling me that if I went down to that store clerk with your picture,

-279-

he'd say 'Yes, I sold beer to that girl tonight'?"

I remembered what I looked like crying, and crumpled my lower lip, clenched my throat, and blinked. "Yes. The clerk was a short guy with dyed blond hair."

"And he sold it to you, and you walked on campus with it?"

"I jumped over the stone fence, I didn't go past the guard," I sniffled. "I'm such a jerk, I know. Demi had no idea I was bringing it up here. Really, he didn't."

I stole a glance at Demi. He was looking at me, astonished.

And then I burst into tears. Real or faked, I wasn't entirely sure.

WHAT HAPPENED was, they kicked me out. The next morning, Demi and I had to see Morales, Reanne, and the summer institute secretary at an eight a.m. meeting in the administrative offices, for purposes of disciplinary action. But Demi was let off with a slap on the wrist and an admonition not to let his high spirits get the better of his judgment, while I took the fall.

Morales said he'd had reports from Farrell that

I'd been in the boys' dorm after hours earlier in the summer. Reports from Reanne that I was disruptive in rehearsal. He'd found me combative in Acting, and in general, my attitude had been blatant disrespect for the summer institute and all it stood for. I was eroding the morale of the community. Now they'd found me bringing illegal beverages onto campus and getting other underage people to drink them.

They had already called my parents. I was going home that afternoon.

Yes, performances were in six days, but they'd work another actor in for both *Midsummer* and *Cats*. Reanne said she was sorry, but she knew I hadn't been happy here, and even *Cats* hadn't made me happy, so maybe this was a sign that Wildewood wasn't the best place for me after all, and the universe was sending my consciousness a message.

Morales said he found my behavior unacceptable.

DEMI HUGGED me and said he was sorry we had our Third Official Quarrel and forget every awful thing he'd said, he didn't mean it, he really didn't mean a word of it. We would never quarrel again, would we? Never. And I was the most incredible girl. I didn't have to do it. I knew that, right? Did I want him to tell Morales the truth? Because he still could.

No, no, of course not.

Did I know how much he loved me? More than chocolate cake, more than sex, more than Liza Minnelli.

Yes, I knew.

"You're my total savior and I owe you," said Demi, having walked me to the door of my dorm room. "Anything you ever need, you tell me."

I said not to worry. I hadn't belonged at Wildewood in the first place, probably.

But then I burst into tears.

I was Rumpleteazer, after all. I would miss being Rumpleteazer.

I couldn't believe I was going to miss being Rumpleteazer.

And Theo. I would miss—I didn't even know what it was I would miss, with Theo. Something I'd never had before.

I would miss doing vocal warm-ups before a show. Putting on makeup. I would miss the Advanced Dance evening presentation with live drummers, and the Stage Combat demonstration in which I was scheduled to single-handedly defeat six boys, fighting first with swords and then with bare hands.

I'd miss hearing Candie sing "Somewhere That's Green." Nanette as Julie in *Show Boat*. Iz and Demi in *Bye Bye Birdie*.

I would miss seeing Lyle in his donkey's head and unitard.

I would miss the show-offy competitiveness. The big personalities. The smell of the rehearsal studios, the costumes hanging in the hallways, piano music from behind every door. The glitter and the sweat.

"We'll miss *you*," said Demi. "It won't be the same without you here."

I SPENT THE morning packing my bags. I talked to my father briefly on the telephone. He was stern, but not too mad. I had never been in any trouble before, and it is always hard to get him to emote. He did seem surprised at this new development, but ah well, there are always bumps in the road, and no use getting too dramatic about them as they're not the end of the world.

He said he was coming to get me in the van and would be there around one o'clock if there wasn't any traffic.

* * *

AT LUNCHTIME, I told people I was leaving. I hugged everyone good-bye: my roommates, Jade, Starveling, Flute, Snug, and Snout. Theo kissed my neck and said he'd write.

I cried some more and told myself over and over that I'd made the right decision. Then Demi and Lyle walked me out of the cafeteria to get my stuff, and insisted on carrying my bags out to the driveway near the front gate.

My dad drove up. He got out and shook hands with the boys. I heaved my bags into the backseat and got in.

They waved at me as we went down the long, curved driveway. Lyle and Demi, Demi and Lyle.

I tried not to be jealous.

Before Dad drove out of the gate, they had already turned around. They didn't want to be late for afternoon rehearsal.

(click)

> **Sadye:** It's August first, and we're in the car going back to Ohio. I have been kicked out of Wildewood for buying a six-pack-- but really for being opinionated.

Or disrespectful. Or not good
enough. I don't know which.

Can I just say? It is one thing to
be heroic in the moment, and
another to take the real
consequence and go back to
Brenton when everyone else gets
to stay, including your new
almost-boyfriend.

Mr. Paulson (*driving*): You were
coming back in eight days,
anyhow. I had it on my
calendar.

Sadye: That's not the point, Dad.

Mr. Paulson: Sarah, why are you so
down about Brenton all the time?
We have a nice life there.

Sadye: It's fine, Dad.

Mr. Paulson: You talk like it's
prison, when we have a yard and
three bedrooms.

Sadye: I said, it's fine.

Mr. Paulson: Your mother and I
thought you'd be happy if you
went away to this drama program;
we only sent you because we
thought you'd like it, and then
you go making trouble.

Sadye: I'm sorry, Dad. I know I wasted your money.

Mr. Paulson: *(keeps driving)*

Sadye: Can I go in the backseat, Dad?

Mr. Paulson: You're gonna climb over while I'm on the interstate?

Sadye: Yeah, I'll just have the seat belt off for a second.

Mr. Paulson: Okay. But don't kick me as you climb over. I'm going fifty-five, here.

(shuffle, bang, shuffle, bang)

Sadye: *(whispering)* Okay, I'm in the backseat. Dad just shoved a CD in the stereo and it's *Cabaret*.

Mr. Paulson: This has been in the car since I drove you up. It's actually pretty good! I've listened to it a few times. This "Wilkommen" song is in German and French, did you know that? He's saying "bienvenue." That's "welcome" in French.

Sadye: It's not pretty good, Dad.

Mr. Paulson: What?

Sadye: It's insanely brilliant. Not pretty good.

Mr. Paulson: Okay, okay. I just thought I'd tell you I liked it.

Sadye: *(whispering again)* I keep telling myself I did the right thing. I saved Demi and me, right? I saved us. I saved him.

Because a friendship, a real friendship, should survive all the stuff that comes at it-- boyfriends and competition and different opinions and secrets. Shouldn't it?

Demi Howard is my best friend, so it's okay to tell a lie to keep him in school; it's good to make a sacrifice. That's what he would do for me.

All right. Maybe he wouldn't.

But that's the point, too. You can't only do things because you know you'll get a return on it later. You have to do them out of generosity. Be bighearted because you are, not because someone will pay you back somehow.

Anyway, it was worth it. Because
    we were in the worst quarrel
    we'd ever had--the kind where
    maybe you're not friends
    anymore afterward--and now
    we're not. Now it's good
    between us and I won't lose
    him.
(pause, *tinny sound of Minnelli
    singing "Maybe This Time" on the
    stereo*)
I think that's the end of this
    tape. Bye.
(*shuffle, click*)

Bᴜᴛ I ᴅɪᴅ lose Demi.

Home in Brenton, I spent August lying on the couch and complaining of the heat, wishing Theo would write me like he said he would, and wondering why he'd never responded to the postcard I'd sent.

I watched the clock go around. I slept. My dad, to give him credit, bought me a big photographic history of Broadway and tried to pull me out of my funk by renting *Moulin Rouge* and corralling us into "family movie night." But I hated watching a musical with my parents; they weren't going to wear *Moulin Rouge* outfits with me the next day, or replay "Lady Marmalade" six times and dance around the living room, or dissect Nicole Kidman's shoddy dancing skills, the way Demi would have done. The way Nanette, Lyle, or Iz would have done. Or even Candie.

I mean, my dad had never even heard of Nicole Kidman before he saw the movie.

I spent the fall attending Brenton High, eating lunch by myself. I went back to classes at Miss Delilah's, but I couldn't bring myself to tell her and Mr. Trocadero I'd been expelled from Wildewood, so I stopped hanging around after class was over. I took a weekend job at a drugstore to fill the empty hours, and lived for the bursts of song that were Demi's sloppily written e-mails and occasional photographs.

He didn't come home until winter break, and when he got there, several inches taller and with his hair grown into a halo of fuzzy locks, he spent half the time on his cell to Lyle.

We did have our usual adventures. We put the Christmas tree ornaments into pornographic positions with each other, and my parents didn't notice. We built a snowman that looked like Liza Minnelli until one of its arms fell off, and then we called it Lopsided Liza. We choreographed a dance number that went up and down my block in the snow, and convinced my father to trail after us with his video camera, documenting it for posterity.

But we weren't together in the same way. Demi lived at Wildewood, soaked in theater and love. He had been in *Romeo and Juliet* (Mercutio), *Sweet Charity* (Daddy) and *Master Harold and the Boys* (Willie), just since September, and he was taking acting, theater history, and lighting design, in addition to academics and private voice instruction. He and Lyle had broken up for a week around Thanksgiving—but were back together now. He wore a watch Lyle had given him—an early Christmas present—and talked in that "we" speak, the way couples do, where there's no reason to even ask who "we" is, because "we" is always the same two people. "We borrowed a car from this guy Fernando and drove into the city," he'd say. Or "We found a way to get on the roof of the dance studio again. You sneak out the fourth-floor classroom window and go up the fire escape. No one ever locks it."

He asked me about my life, but there wasn't much to tell. It was razzle-dazzle deprived—no getting around it. "My mother decided to feature both the red and the yellow kitchen timers in the holiday catalog!" I shouted with as much excitement as I could fake. "My father's tennis game has improved! I have a new bedspread! I got

a B-minus in gym for never wearing knee-high socks!"
Then I sang,

> *Knee-high socks are not for me,*
> *My calves and ankles want to breathe, you see!*
> *The knee-high socks are a fashion don't,*
> *They can dock me down a grade, but I just won't . . .*
> *Wear knee-high socks!*
> *Oh, knee-high socks!*
> *I tell you in my own defense,*
> *That I shall make a stand against*
> *Those knee-high soooooooocks!*

He did laugh—he was always my best audience—but I noticed Demi didn't talk to me much about his dreams for the future. I knew he was applying to Carnegie Mellon, NYU, and Juilliard (his first choice), because his parents discussed it when I went there for dinner. But he skirted around the subject with me, as if he were scared to ask what I wanted, now that I'd been somehow excluded from wanting what he did—because both of us knew I didn't have it in me.

He loved me. I know he did.

And he probably always will.

But Demi doesn't need me now, at all.

* * *

AFTER THE winter holidays, Demi left to go back to Wildewood.

Something changed in me then. Like I wasn't waiting for him to come home anymore. He might return the next summer, or he might not. Maybe he'd be looking for a New York apartment with Lyle. In any case, he'd always be visiting.

We'd never be home together again, and nothing would ever be quite the same as it was.

I SHOULD tell you what happened to everyone after I left Wildewood. Demi and Lyle called me after the performance weekend and gave me the rundown of all the shows.

Birdie was the smash of the summer. Demi, Iz, and the other leads were personally congratulated by Morales afterward. *Show Boat* was old-fashioned but Nanette was great. *Cats* was better than anyone had thought it could be. And *A Midsummer Night's Unitard* was a tangled two hours of pretension and Lycra that fully rivaled *Bedsheet Oedipus* in laughability. Even Lyle's boatload of talent couldn't save it.

The only upside was that Starveling didn't faint.

Despite some continued difficulties with the mechanics of the giant man-eating plant in *Little Shop*, Candie's crystal soprano broke everyone's hearts. She went back home to New Jersey happy and well-assured of her cherries jubileeishness. Nanette told me the *Jekyll* poster came down once the dentist said the L-word, and Candie and her boyfriend went home promising to write every day.

She sent me a card in September with a picture of Jesus on it, saying they'd all missed me and now she was playing Laurie in her school production of *Oklahoma!*

I didn't know what to say, writing back, so I drew a goofy sketch of her in a gingham dress and a cowgirl hat, kissing Hugh Jackman as Curly. Not that I'm that good of an artist, but I labeled all the parts of the drawing so she could tell what it was supposed to be.

Candie never wrote back.

It's funny that someone you lived with for a whole summer could disappear out of your life; someone you saw naked, someone who told you all about her inner life, even when you didn't want to know, someone meek who turned out to be someone brave.

Funny how suddenly, there's not too much information—there's none.

Nanette went home and slept on her parents' couch for a couple weeks, and did a callback audition for *The Secret Garden* in New York. She e-mailed me that her dad was barely talking to her—they hadn't driven out to see *Show Boat* because her sister was in callbacks for a film—but when she got the role of Mary Lennox, he loosened up. With Nanette's family, a lead role at La Jolla erases a lot of sins.

Within a week, she'd been shipped out to California with her Professional Children's School laptop, where instead of living in theater-sponsored rental apartments like the other actors from out of town, she lived with Iz and her family in downtown San Diego. Iz found out that Nanette was coming and invited her; Nanette was grateful because she didn't want to live alone.

Once she was there, Nanette e-mailed me that nothing Iz had said about herself at the start of Wildewood was true. She didn't go to a specialized arts high school; just an ordinary public school. She took dance classes at the local Jewish community center and private voice once a week. She hadn't been in *Born Yesterday*, *Kiss Me Kate*, or *Damn Yankees*, and she'd never drooled on herself during auditions. Her school didn't allow anyone to even try out for the plays until they were seniors. What's more, Wolf—Iz's older boyfriend with the motorcycle—didn't exist.

Iz broke down and confessed all this two days after

Nanette arrived, saying she'd wanted Nanette to stay with her so badly she'd decided it was worth coming clean.

"I picked her up at school on Monday when I didn't have rehearsal," wrote Nanette, "and she was standing there alone, not talking to anyone. I think she's kind of a freak at school. Like nobody knows what to make of her. When she got in the car—that's when she told me. I guess because I saw her standing there by herself. Next week she's coming up to watch a rehearsal at La Jolla."

I was furious at Iz for lying to us. I couldn't believe Nanette was so mellow about it, though I guess I understood, since she was practically being adopted by Iz's family. I stomped around and complained to my mother.

"But didn't you do the same thing?" she asked me.

"No."

"It seems to me you did."

Since when did my mother get analytical about my life? Since when was she even focusing on anything to do with anything besides kitchen gadgets? "I never lied," I told her.

"Of course not."

"She was operating under false pretenses. She lied to everyone for three consecutive summers."

"That's not what I meant, anyway," my mother said. "I meant, you reinvented yourself—when you first tried out for Wildewood. Cut your hair. Got all those new clothes. Changed your name."

"Oh."

"Your friend Isadora"—my mother spelled the name out with her hand—"did the same thing you did."

"Not exactly the same," I argued. "In fact, not the same at all. Because she *lied*."

"Fine." My mother sighed. "I need to check my e-mail. Something's coming in from work." She opened her laptop on the kitchen table, moving her eyes away from me so she couldn't read my lips or see me sign.

I went into the living room and put *Wicked* on the CD player, skipping ahead to "Popular," and putting it on repeat.

AN HOUR LATER, I realized I wasn't mad anymore. I went to the drugstore and bought a bunch of silly presents to make a care package for Iz and Nanette. Paper crowns, some glitter lip gloss, a paperback romance novel with racy bits, a package of water balloons, and a box of Oreos. I packed it all up in bubble wrap.

Hey, Wonder Women.

Did I ever tell you that home in Brenton my name used to be Sarah? Well, it was. And I hated it.

So I changed it to Sadye. But I never told anyone at Wildewood.

Anyway, since you guys were my best friends there, I wanted you to know.

Hope you are POUNCING as much as possible in your spare time. Brenton sucks the suckiness of Suckville, and I miss you both.

XO

Sadye.

AKA Sarah.

AKA Peter Quince.

AKA Tall Hot Box.

AKA Mint Chocolate Chip

P.S. Read page 159 of the enclosed book if you need instructions on the jumbo pounce.

FOR A WHILE after that, we e-mailed every couple days—but when Nanette went into tech rehearsals for *Secret Garden*, our correspondence petered out, and I didn't hear from them all winter and spring.

I SENT THEO a postcard I found of Marlon Brando as Sky Masterson in the movie of *Guys and Dolls*—and gave him my e-mail address.

Like I said, he didn't reply.

I don't know what I would have done if he had, anyway. It wasn't like we could go out long distance. But I also couldn't believe he just disappeared out of my life. As if we'd never kissed.

Still, he was the first boy who found me a pounce-able, deliciously mint-chocolate-chip girl. To James, I was someone who was there, in the moonlight or on the dance floor. I could have been anyone. We hadn't really talked.

But Theo got me. So I know there are people who do. Get me. Even if they're hundreds of miles away.

THE END is in sight now. The end of Ohio, I mean. The end of this razzle-dazzle–deprived town.

This is my senior year, and after graduation I am going to get out of Brenton and out of this quiet house and out of the suffocating sameness, and I will never look back.

No one here is going to save me. I haven't heard from Demi in months.

So I am going to save myself.

I know what I think is good, and why. Though not everyone will always agree with me.

I think of things—like singing on the roof, or "Supercalifragilisticexpialidocious" at the break of dawn, or people being flavors of ice cream, or staging *Midsummer* in a forest of roses.

I see stage pictures in my mind. And sometimes dances. *Godspell Pillowcase. Sexy Fiddler.*

I make up songs and people laugh. I am bossy and outspoken.

I am physically strong and even imposing.

I am kind when people need it, though maybe not always. When things are broken, I can see how they might be fixed.

I am not afraid to ask questions, and I am not afraid to make people angry.

I have these talents in me, though I may not have a voice made for singing or a disposition for acting.

I am Sadye Paulson, even if some people do call me Sarah, and there is bigness inside of me. So I will figure out what to do with it.

I have to.

I will.

Epilogue

TRANSCRIPT of a telephone conversation, June 12th, nearly a year after the summer at Wildewood:

Demi: Monsieur le petit Howard, at your service.

Sadye: Demi, it's me.

Demi: Miss Sadye! It's been like three months--no, four, I think.

Sadye: I know!

Demi: Sorry I didn't call you back.

Sadye: S'okay. Forget about it.

Demi: No, really, I'm sorry. That was lame. I let life get away from me.

Sadye: Listen, I'm calling you now because--

Demi: Oh, wait, before you get into that. You won't believe where I am right now.

Sadye: Where?

Demi: The center of the world.

Sadye: Where?

Demi: Forty-second Street. New York City. I swear to you, I am looking at the *Lion King* poster on the front of the theater.

Sadye: No way.

Demi: It's true!

Sadye: No, I mean, you won't believe where *I* am right now. I am looking at the face of Nanette Watson on this like, enormous *Secret Garden* poster. That's why I called you.

Demi: What? Where? What poster?

Sadye: I'm on Broadway and Forty-sixth.

Demi: You are *not*.

Sadye: Oh, but I *am*.

Demi: You're like, four blocks away! Ahhhh! Lyle--wait, Sadye, Lyle wandered off, oh there he is--Lyle! Sadye is on the phone and she's at--what?

Sadye: Broadway and Forty-sixth.

Demi: *(to Lyle)* Looking at a picture of Nanette Watson on Broadway! No, I'm not lying.

Sadye: What did he say?

Demi: He doesn't believe me. Stay where you are. Okay, we're walking north. Oops, wait, we have to go the other direction. No, Lyle! Okay, now we're walking north. Don't move! We're going to be there in like two minutes.

Sadye: We have to get tickets. Wait. Why are you here? I had no idea you were going to be here.

Demi: We're staying with Lyle's brother till I can get into the dorms in September.

Sadye: For Juilliard?

Demi: No, those fools didn't let me in. I'm going to NYU. It'll be okay. Lyle's going to Carnegie Mellon. Wait, why are *you* here?

Sadye: I got a summer internship with New York Theatre Workshop.

Assisting the assistant artistic
director.

Demi: Getting coffee?

Sadye: Exactly. And it doesn't
pay, so I'm waiting tables in
the evenings.

Demi: Still, that's cool.

Sadye: I'm cat-sitting for this
banking friend of my dad's who's
at his country house for the
summer.

Demi: Okay, we're on Broadway and
Forty-fifth now.

Sadye: Oh, I'm so excited. The box
office is open. Should we buy
tickets?

Demi: Yes. Can you go tonight?
Wait--oh, what? Lyle wants to
go too.

Sadye: Excellent.

Demi: Okay, oh, is that you in the
red skirt? I think I see you,
but I'm not sure.

Sadye: Reddish-pinkish skirt.

Demi: Okay, here I am, I'm waving.

Sadye: I'm hanging up now. Oh,
there you are!

Demi: Lyle, there she is.

Sadye: You wave funny. Do you know that? You've got to work on your wave.

Demi: I see you! I see you!

Sadye: I see you, too.

Appendixes

1. Wondering what to watch? Here are Sadye's favorite movie musicals:

West Side Story unrated

Cabaret PG

Chicago PG-13

Singin' in the Rain G

Hair PG

Fame R

Grease PG

Little Shop of Horrors PG-13

Sweet Charity G

Kiss Me Kate unrated

Damn Yankees unrated

2. To hear some of the songs Sadye talks about in this book, go to www.theboyfriendlist.com

Look at the right column and find Sadye's iMix. You can download the playlist into iTunes or another MP3 player.

3. Wildewood Academy does not exist. I made it up, along with all its faults. However, I did go to three years of summer drama camp, five hundred years ago. The schools to which I went shall remain nameless, and one of them has closed down. If you're interested in attending a summer theater camp, the following are the best known:

- Stagedoor Manor, www.stagedoormanor.com
- The National High School Institute at Northwestern University, www.northwestern.edu/nhsi/
- Interlochen Arts Academy, www.interlochen.org

Acknowledgments

THANK YOU a zillion times to Benjamin Ellis Fine, for letting me steal his drama school anecdotes for this book, and for taking the time to tell them to me. I have transfigured many a Ben Fine story in these pages. There are also several other people who shared their stories and feelings about acting at my request: in particular, Lisa Burdige, Jenna Jolley, Rebecca Soler, Trevor Williams, and Ayun Halliday.

Many thanks to my agent, Elizabeth Kaplan, because she is awesome. And to my editor, Donna Bray, who took me out to lunch, listened to several ridiculous stories about unitards—and signed me up to write this book, pushing me to make it better and better through more drafts than it should have taken. Also to Brenda Bowen, Arianne Lewin, Emily Schultz, and everyone at

Hyperion, especially designer Beth Clark, who worked so hard on the jacket.

Novelist Maryrose Wood endured several e-mails in which I probed her exquisitely theatrical brain for tidbits, trivia, and ideas. She also read a first draft with great insight. Zoe Jenkin answered questions about *Wicked* and *Rent* and other shows about which she is far more expert than I. She also took me to see Kristin at Carnegie Hall, and *Wicked* on Broadway (though Big Len paid for the tickets—thank you!), and she kept me company for a number of other, less thrilling, productions.

Some years ago, the members and leaders of the BMI Musical Theater Workshop gave me a four-year education in musical theater history and writing that can't be beat. I hope they will not hold the meatball, knee-high, and Tyrannosaurus rex songs against me too much. The members of my YA novelists newsgroup contributed real and thoughtful comments on the question of talent and the appeal of the theater world, helping me sort out what I wanted to say.

My parents paid for me to go to summer drama camp for three years, and always encouraged my theatrical endeavors despite a relatively obvious lack of talent. My father took me to see *West Side Story*, *Peter Pan*, *Cats*, and *Annie* on Broadway and introduced me to cast

albums for *Hair* and *Guys and Dolls* (among others)—
little dreaming what a monster he was creating.

My husband endured the David Hasselhoff *Jekyll & Hyde* without complaint. I don't think I can convey his support any more succinctly than that.